TITLE :

RUN WITH THE PACK

AUTHOR :

FARHAN ILYAS

Chapter 1

"Muuuum, I'm eager," groaned seven-year-old Mikey
from the rearward sitting arrangement of our old, beat-up car. A second
afterward, his grouching was upheld by a boisterous thunder of
his vacant stomach, which overwhelmed even the
motor's thunder and radio's breaking. We had lost the
signal around thirty minutes prior, yet nobody had at this point
tried to switch the gadget off.

"We'll before long show up at Redforest," expressed mum, gripping
the wheel with such a lot of power, her knuckles turned
white. She tossed me an unhinged look, and I swallowed, feeling
the too recognizable fingers of fear bending my
internal parts. Of late, a basic "I'm eager" unnerved me more
than a blood and gore movie night.
"Josie will check assuming that we actually have a few chocolate bars left
in the glove compartment," Mum added, brushing endlessly
her oily, dull earthy colored hair at the rear of the chaotic
bun. She got her little finger on an old, grimy clinical
fix that covered portion of her face and concealed four spiked,
recuperating paw marks under.
What's more, to imagine that main seven days prior, mum wouldn't have
allow us to take off from the house with a spot of soil...

In any case, there was no house like there was no food in the
glove compartment. The last chocolate bar had evaporated
about an hour prior in the wretched profundities of Mikey's
stomach. Yet, I scrounged through the crate in any case -
more for the good of mum than in trusts I would, by some
supernatural occurrence, track down anything there.
Mum tossed me another speedy look, and I shook my
head just somewhat, pressing together my lips. I felt her
alarm rising - the bitter smell of her perspiration filled the vehicle,
gradually aggravating me, hence, Mikey.
"What's that smell?" The youngster asked, fixing in his
seat. His large, green eyes shined shockingly in the semidarkness that encompassed us, and his noses erupted in a
amusing, carnal way.
A baaaaaad sign.
I rifled through the pockets of my long, earthy colored sweater
nibbled all the more quickly now, and found a scrunched,
half-eaten granola I had totally overlooked.
"Gotcha!" I shouted energetically, waving the thing in the
air victoriously, to which mum breathed out a murmur of help
also, apparently quieted down. The smell of dread died down,
also, Mikey's eyes lost their frightfully sparkle.
I pivoted, grinning as I unsettled the mop of his
oily, rosy earthy colored hair. "Try not to gag, you covetousguts!" I chuckled,
gazing directly into his human, green
irises. Mikey maintained eye contact with me for unequivocally two seconds

before he looked away. He did that a great deal of late. Yet
of late, we as a whole did a great deal of unusual things.
"Much appreciated, Jo," he said unobtrusively.
"Try also it," I waved him off and turned around
around.
Mum looked at me, mumbling a soundless "Thank
you," her eyes loaded with unshed tears. I grinned week by week and
shrugged.
One fire put out - a billion to go.
As she zeroed in back out and about once more, I murmured, inclining
my head on the rest while we passed a
bombastic sign "Welcome to Redforest. Populace 500."
I shut my eyes.
I had never been more joyful at seeing such
Frightfulness.

Chapter 2

"That man smells like us," murmured Mikey looking at the shop aide of the little gas station we halted by to snatch a few tidbits.

The station was situated in no place, and it was encircled by dull, unpleasant timberland from each side. In any case, it was the main spot we had seen that offered any food since we had passed the appalling greeting sign, which was around 30 minutes prior - not that I had been counting...

"Try not to gaze; it's discourteous," I chid my sibling, overlooking his remark as I squeezed the hot cocoa button on the espresso candy machine.

I made a respectable attempt not to ponder what the kid had recently said. As opposed to the seven-year-old, I denied to concede I saw the arrangement of exceptional abilities I had abruptly gained later, indeed, that evening.

Mikey complied with me, promptly getting keen on the sacks of jams before him. I shook my head, scowling. Because of reasons simply known to my sibling, he begun to pay attention to me more than our mum.

I gave Mikey hot cocoa and squeezed a latte button, looking at the clerk gabbing with mum.

He was an immense person, fabricated like a tank, with arms the size

of congested watermelons. His face, canvassed in a

to some degree shaggy, earthy colored facial hair, held the edge of

pertinacity and inflexibility normally connected with individuals

living in the brutal climate. In spite of that, his

chocolate-earthy colored eyes were shockingly delicate.

"Long excursion?" I heard him ask as he proceeded to

pack some food into the plastic sack. He didn't actually

remark on mum's grimy careful fix, our questionable

condition of cleanliness, or dark circles under our eyes that

saved just Mikey. As though the person saw solitary ladies

with two children seeming to be the survivors of homegrown

savagery on the run consistently. Perhaps he did. He worked

at a gas station all things considered.

"You can't really understand... Ben," Mum moaned sleepily, perusing

the man's name on the plate joined to his blue shirt.

"Me and the children need just to stop

some place warm with a fair shower and perfect, hot

water and have a decent night's rest

"Do you have a spot to remain?"

Mum piece her lip and grimaced.

"The issue lies with indeed, that... We didn't want to stop on our

way to Dover Hill, yet I'm so worn out I can scarcely keep my

eyes open. The children could utilize some rest as well," she

made sense of, murmuring quietly.

6

Ben didn't look shocked.

"Assuming that is the situation, I realize the spot you're not kidding,"

Ben said, giving mum a green leaflet. "My sister

runs a motel. Nothing extravagant, granted, however it has all you

need, and Rosie, that is her name, incidentally, is an extraordinary

cook, on the off chance that I might say so myself. Also, assuming you tell her I've sent

you, she'll give you a markdown."

"That sounds promising," Mum laughed. It was even

real. "Sit back and relax - we won't scam you. Really we don't

plan to remain long."

"Quit worrying about that." Ben waved mum off. "Do you come

from far?" He asked in an apparently detached way. If it

wasn't for the new advancements in my body, I

could not have possibly singled out the slight flash of interest

there. Mum certainly didn't.

So I chose to utilize that exact second to approach the

counter and hand mum her beverage.

"Here," I said, peering toward the man with alert.

He figured out my dubious look and offered me a

expansive grin that transformed him into a major teddy bear. All things considered,

OK, a wild bear.

I felt myself become flushed a bit, and I bit within my

cheek, detecting this intuitive inclination to drop my look. It

was odd on the grounds that I could never depict myself as

shy. I attempted to battle my peculiar response, however I surrendered

following two seconds, zeroing in on mum all things being equal. She looked

the most loosened up I had seen her in a long time, and I wasn't

sure in the event that I loved the reality it was Ben who made her lower

her watchman so immediately like that. He was only an outsider. On the off

 chance that

Mikey was correct and that man resembled us - and by

us, he implied himself and me - it would mean Ben...

"Much thanks to you, sweety. Ben here has suggested us a

dwelling house," Mum took me back to the present. I

squinted. "Furthermore, prepare to have your mind blown. We have a

 rebate!" She

added far over too merrily.

"Um, no doubt, that is perfect," I grinned, faking energy.

"In any case, Mikey and I are going to make a beeline for the vehicle,"

I pointed in the unpleasant heading of our truck. "You know,

on the off chance that you wondered..."

"Goodness, alright. I'll be right behind you. Do you have keys? I

still need to pay for our beverages and the remainder of the

food..."

"Sit back and relax, I have them with me," I tapped the right

pocket of my green plane coat and turned around,

prepared to set out toward the entryways.

That was the point at which I felt it - a delicate mix in the air that brought

Ben's aroma straightforwardly to my nose. I was unable to imagine any longer. My younger sibling was correct - that person smelled

like us. It was a peculiar combination of wood, fuel, musk

furthermore, something strangely recognizable, something that reminded

me of that bad dream of a night when the crap hit the

Fan..

My eyes snapped to the person behind the counter, and I

froze, feeling my heartbeat getting as globules of nervous perspiration

begun to assemble on my brow. Ben's noses erupted,

what's more, he took a whiff, his eyes broadening somewhat. The

development was scarcely there, yet I saw it.

I saw it...

"Easy..." He mumbled soothingly, his voice excessively low for

human ears to get it, for mum to get it. She was

too bustling requesting headings to pay us any brain

However, not Mikey.

"Josie?" His restless voice slice through the strain like a

blade through margarine. "Are you alright?" He murmured,

moving toward me. He pulled me by my hand, requesting

my consideration as he gave me a stressed look.

"Y-Yeah," I made a sound as if to speak and constrained a grin. Really I
didn't

need to scare the kid considerably further. God just knew,

of late he flipped out when terrified or vexed. I most

most certainly didn't need the episode with the TV to

repeat... "Come, we really want to go. Mum's nearly

wrapped up."

I immediately pulled my sibling by his hand and as distant
from the more unusual as could be expected. I swore I could feel Ben's
look on the rear of my head in any event, when the ways to the
shop shut behind us.

Chapter 3

Twenty minutes and five sausages later, question broke
mum's determination.
"You sure we're on the correct way?" She asked, inclining
on the wheel while attempting to see something through the
thick haze that had crawled on us.
"That is what the guide says..." I expressed, following the line
Ben drew for mum with a dark marker. "It would be ideal for we to see
the sign right about... presently," I added, easing up, as I
at long last seen the goddamn thing somewhere far off. "We
need to take the following turn."
"Left or right?"
"Left and onto the country road."
"Beneficial thing somewhere around one of us has youthful eyes. I would
have missed the sign if..."
"Keep an eye out!" I shouted out.
Mum unexpectedly stirred things up around town, and I was thrown forward
then drove once again by the belt that horrendously dove in my
chest as we halted two feet from a goliath wolf
that unexpectedly jumped before us.

It was greater than nature ought to permit thus dull dark

it was practically dark with a bit of white around its

snuggle. I felt as opposed to saw mum gripping my hand

what's more, her nails penetrated my skin, the coppery smell of

blood filling the vehicle very quickly, nonetheless, I

disregarded it, zeroed in exclusively on the peril in front. The

monster respected us cooly with its wise, glimmering,

golden eyes. I sucked in a breath when those spheres

arrived on me, the power of the look choking out me for

an excruciatingly lengthy second before the creature looked

away and similarly as unexpectedly evaporated in the shrubs.

"Jo? Is everything alright?" Mikey's lethargic voice cut the

quietness in the vehicle.

"Great overall's. Return to rest," I said, my voice still precarious.

Mum changed the gear and began the vehicle, murmuring

delicately, "One evening. We're remaining in only for one evening,

and afterward we're out of this goddamn opening."

I can't help but concur.

* * *

We actually needed to drive for quite a while before a gigantic

dwelling house rose before us, its warm yellow lights

directing us like signals.

"Assuming that is not a lot, I don't have any idea, what is..." I

murmured in wonder, taking in the structure in front - its

gigantic patio, fieldstone wrapping the ground floor,

honey-earthy colored logs making up the main floor, and
lovely nature-themed carvings enhancing wooden
pointed curved windows.

Mum put the vehicle in leave.

"I bet they have boiling water here," she expressed, looking at the
working from behind the windscreen, no less intrigued
than I was.

"Furthermore, no bugs... or on the other hand mice," I kidded however
thought twice about it a
second some other time when I saw the expression all over.

"Goodness honey, I'm so sorry..." She stifled out, concealing her
face in her grasp. "I know it's been poo on you of late
with what has befallen your father and presently... presently...
this... furthermore, I'm heartbroken, but..."

"Mum, please, don't..." I asked. "What has been going on with father
isn't your fault..."

"Be that as it may, it is," she murmured, removing me with a far off
appearance all over. I realized the sentence wasn't
implied for my ears, so I didn't quick her, not actually
sure assuming I was prepared to find one more skeleton in the
storeroom. Mum made a sound as if to speak and detached her seat
belt. "In any case, enough of that. How about we simply look at this spot
up. I frantically need that hot shower Ben has
guaranteed us."

"Better believe it, me as well," I concurred gradually, watching mum rush out
of the vehicle.

Might it be said that she was at long last losing it?

Might it be said that we weren't all?

I followed her with my eyes as she went down the

rock way towards the entryway patio on which a lady

showed up - Rosie, on the off chance that what Ben said was right. She was

wearing a couple of dim, agreeable workout pants, a

matching hoodie and appeared to be somewhat anxious to welcome

mum. The two ladies traded merriments quickly

also, continued on toward casual chitchat, so I pivoted to check

on Mikey once more.

He was all the while dozing so I just delicately brushed away a

stray keep of his rosy earthy colored hair and escaped the

truck.

The cool night air attacked me very quickly,

gnawing my cheeks. I shuddered, set my hands under my

armpits in a frantic endeavor to keep warm, then, at that point,

headed towards the boot to get our effects. Not

that we had a lot. Mum had pressed us all carelessly, as it were

taking the necessities. Our baggage comprised of one

huge bag and my calfskin knapsack.

I tossed the sack behind me then, heaving, put the

weighty bag on the rock carport, abruptly feeling

the evening glow all over. Naturally, I

gazed toward the moon's bow, quietly counting the

days that isolated me from the full moon and my

unavoidable destruction.

Assuming that legends were valid, I had just two additional long stretches of mankind ahead - except if the fix worked.

All things considered, poop.

I frowned then headed towards the visiting ladies. The sound of rock moving under the soles of my coaches alarmed them both to my presence. They turned to confront me.

"Josie, meet Mrs. Davies," mum said, grinning.

I straightened out the sack's stripe and held out my hand in the lady's heading. From very close, she looked even more lovely than I accepted. She was on a unimposing side, had bourbon earthy colored hair restricted in a long, chaotic french twist, large yellow-earthy colored eyes, a little, delicately improved nose, and heart-molded lips. She additionally possessed a scent like us, however my response to her was basically unique in relation to it was to Ben. There was something about the lady that quieted the tempest seething inside me.

I didn't have the foggiest idea what to consider it.

Mrs. Davis shook my hand and grinned as she said, "Exquisite to meet you, Josie. I'm Rosalynd, yet you can call me Rose."

"The joy's mine Mrs. Da... erm... Rose..." I answered ungracefully, again feeling this bizarre impulse to look away from her agreeable however serious look. I needed to battle with myself to keep my eyes straight. I even oversaw -

some way or another - for pitful four seconds before mum saved

my pride and gave me a reason to zero in on something

else.

"Josie, perhaps Rose could show you around while I'll

get Mikey from the car...?" She inquired.

"Um, no doubt, okay..." I said, lifting our stuff.

"Hey now then," Rosalynd empowered cheerfully,

motioning for me to follow. I did exactly that, climbing the

steps as she began to make sense of, "Today's somewhat tranquil,

be that as it may, generally we have loads of individuals in. I truly want to
believe that you don't

mind."

We went inside the structure and into the long, brilliant,

tight corridor.

"Actually no, not by any stretch of the imagination. In any case, we will not
be remaining long."

"That is a disgrace. Where are you going to?" Rosalynd

went straight for one more stairwell and begun to

climb them. As I pulled behind her, I got an impression

of an elegantly enriched rural style well known room with

a comfortable looking marble chimney. Some way or another I knew

where I would go through the night - in the event that I didn't

breakdown on the bed face-first.

"Dover Hill... We're going to Dover Hill," I replied, a

bit occupied, as I put the bag on the stained

floor.

"I see," The lady commented in an odd voice. I
overviewed her, yet I was unable to see whatever raised my
doubt. I was really going crazy. "Do you have
family there?" Rose asked, keeping a cordial tone as
she drove me towards the keep going room on the left.
I looked at her again, it was more behind to feel there
the inquiry than straightforward interest.

"Something to that effect," I mumbled after stopping for a moment. I had a
peculiar inclination she wouldn't be satisfied assuming she heard we
were attempting to arrive at the emergency clinic there. However I didn'
know why it even made a difference to me.

Fortunately, Rose didn't proceed with her cross examination. She
pushed the light wooden entryways and reported all things being equal:
"Here is your room."

I wanted to cry. It was the best damn thing I found in a
week, and I wasn't in any event, joking. With how minimal expenditure
we had and how much mum pushed to cover so a lot
distance among us and father at all measure of time
potential, we had spent our evenings any place - for the most part,
nonetheless, in modest, summary inns by the street. This
here felt like an early Christmas present.

"I want to believe that you wouldn't fret how little the room is, yet all at once it's
the greatest accessible one we had for this evening," Mrs. Davis
informed me as we strolled in. I murmured something

cautious, zeroed in on respecting a jumbo bed

covered by the jug green duvet and a beautiful, wooden

closet with cut creature themes on it. They looked

carefully assembled, and I was unable to assist myself with yet drawing nearer

what's more, run a finger on one of the crying wolves. It was so

point by point it nearly appeared to be genuine.

"Pretty, right? My nephew's made the closet all by

himself. He's great with wood, as we like to joke here,"

Rosalynd radiated, her voice loaded proudly.

"It's grand," I murmured, considering what sort of

individual might a kid with abilities at some point as be that.

"Truth be told, a large portion of our furniture was made by him," Mrs.

Davis admitted. "At any rate, I'm boasting once more, and I'm

almost certain you should be worn out. I'll head

first floor. Go ahead and utilize all the gear in our

house and call me in the event that you want anything."

Chapter 4

"Father? Father... I know you're there... Father, please..." I
murmur as the monster's hot breath is fanning my face, its
salvia trickling gradually from its banned teeth.

"Father!"

And afterward there is just torment.

[*]

I awakened with a beginning to the sun sparkling straight in my
face, feeling cold perspiration on my brow and at the scruff
of my neck. Gasping noisily, I sat up and absentmindedly
put my hand on the pulsating, rough scar on the
right half of my stomach. I gradually glanced around, attempting
to fix my hustling beat, just to acknowledge I
was separated from everyone else.

Bizarre.

I unraveled my feet from the duvet and made a beeline for the
stroll in restroom, actually battling to fend off the apparition
of a dream waiting before my eyes. I sprinkled cold
water all over, trusting it could assist me with establishing
myself in the present. Then I tried a look at my
appearance in the mirror.

My look met with two hot, shining circles that
ought to have been hazel yet were for the most part golden, then, at that
point,

immediately moved to my tangled, chestnut hair and pale,

freckled face. I licked the perspiration that assembled over my

lips as tension indeed wound my internal parts. I let out

one more precarious breath, willing my eyes to turn around to

typical. Actually they didn't.

I rushed under a shower.

At the point when I was finished, the restroom was loaded up with steam,

my skin was red, and I was quiet sufficient that my eye

variety got back to business as usual.

I immediately tossed on a dull green hoodie and thin pants

also, left the restroom. As I was en route to put my

make-shift night wear back in the bag, something

attracted me to the window. Without really thinking, I drew nearer and

looked outside at the fall painted woods that

ascended slopes for a significant distance. Some place somewhere out there,

far over the tree crowns, whitish cups of the mountain

tops mixed with the sky blue sky.

Everything appeared to be so tranquil, and my state of mind illuminated a
little...

That is until I seen the recognizable mop of corroded

hair. I noticed Mikey's frantic scramble across the carport,

just to see a kid, or rather, a young fellow I had never

seen previously. Alone. With my sibling.

Goodness, God.

Automatically, I hurried out of the room and flew

ground floor, skirting two stages all at once, nearly

19

colliding with mum on my way. By some supernatural occurrence, she
figured out how to stay away from me, nonetheless, she actually spilled her
newly fermented espresso all around the perfect, wooden floor
what's more, on her fingers. She murmured as she changed her grasp
on the cup and met my terrified look.
"Josie? What's wrong? Are you OK?" The words
left her mouth in a moment, her foreheads wrinkled, stress
wedding her face.
"I've recently seen Mikey outside with a more bizarre," I terminated
out, bothered.
Mum's demeanor transformed into disarray as her strained
body loosened up a little.
"That sounds right, really. He's aiding Rosie's nephew
with the vehicle," She made sense of, attempting to reassure me.
She didn't actually.
"What's more, you let him? Why?! Don't you recollect what
happened two days prior, in the inn? Or on the other hand seven days prior at
the clinic?" I shouted, skeptical. "What if Mikey
blows up or disturb, or...or...?"
"So what was I expected to do, Josie?! Secure him in
the room? Disconnect him from the rest of the world?!" She
shouted out, intruding on me, her voice clearly in the
generally vacant house. "He's just seven..." She gagged
out more delicately now, separating before me.
I nearly lamented my unexpected explosion. Nearly.

"Perhaps wake me up sometime later," I snarled, tossing

my hands up high, baffled at her, at myself, and at

the strangeness of the entire circumstance we found

ourselves in. Without another word, I raged outside,

closing the entryways behind me with a noisy bang.

I rushed onto the rock way, not ready for an

unforeseen surge of cold air that attacked my body and

bit my cheeks. However, the energetic didn't cool me enough,

for I headed towards the young men with restored enthusiasm,

contacting them similarly as Mikey was going to pass the

wrench to the outsider fiddling with the motor.

After hearing me, Mikey halted anything he was

doing, and his head snapped toward me, disarray

damaging his highlights. Seeing me, he illuminated like a

Christmas Tree and ran towards me, yelling my name

as he did. The disturbance drew the consideration of

Rosalynd's nephew, who fixed up from his bowed

position and took a gander at me inquisitively. Our eyes met...

...

...

...

...and afterward Mikey crashed into me at full power,

actually diverting me from the outsider's

mercury irises. I lurched back, on nature wrapping

my hands around my sibling's little structure.

"Yet again jo!" He shouted, giving me one of those

splendid grins of his - so interesting nowadays. No big deal either way

gloomy feelings had driven me outside evaporated that

exact moment. I emptied like an inflatable.

"Prepare to be blown away. Louis' wrecked your record at skipping

stones. He's completed 40 skips! 40! And afterward he showed me

his stunt, and learn to expect the unexpected. I did 15!" He screeched with

energy, pointing at the person, who was currently inclining

on the vehicle's hood with arms got over his

chest.

Getting my dubious look, Louis gave me a fairly

innocent half-grin and gradually lifted his hand in a

welcoming. I felt myself become flushed, light pink unmitigatedly self-
evident

on my generally pale tone, and the kid's smile

developed more extensive, making him much more alluring than he

as of now was. Louis plainly understood what power he had

over me, indeed, most likely over all young ladies, and it made my

acknowledged temper rise. I needed to advise myself that,

anyway attractive Louis was with his dumb grin, stream

dark, french trimmed hair, conditioned body, and awful kid

flows, nothing could and would occur. Not when I was

going to leave unexpectedly early.

"For what reason do you smell like this?" Mikey's abrupt inquiry

diverted me from the outsider. "Is it true or not that you are terrified?"

I peered down at my sibling's scrunched nose and

marginally glimmering eyes. Clearly, my feelings were
inciting the thing inside him.

"I was, however only a tad," I replied, unsettling his hair.

"Why?"

"I had no clue about where you were, so I got a piece stressed," I
made sense of, squatting before him, with the goal that our eyes
were on a similar level. Once more, Mikey wouldn't hold my
look, turning away following a little while. I grimaced,
stressed and a slight bit hurt, however a piece of me was
happy with the kid's response. It was totally confusing. I
didn't have the foggiest idea how I felt any longer.

"Yet, mum realized I was with Louis. She let me," he
whimpered.

"I know, it astonished me, that is all," I grinned at my
sibling, running my hands all over his arms
soothingly. "Will you at last acquaint me with your new
companion?" I redirected the conversation, and my sibling loose
under my touch.

He radiated at me. "Here we go!"

Mikey pulled me towards Louis, then, at that point, halted a couple
pulls back from him. He gestured his head towards
Rosalynd's nephew, his appearance all systematic.

"Josie, this is Louis. Louis, this is my sister Josephine,
however, everybody calls her Josie, or Jo," he said as seriously
as just a seven-year-old would. I was unable to help a grin

23

that lifted the edges of my mouth. Mikey was simply as well

adorable. He helped me to remember the kid from seven days prior, the

one from previously. It made meextremely upset a bit.

"Good to meet you, Josephine, Josie, or Jo," Louis welcomed

me, entertained, joining the demonstration. I understood it was the first

time I had heard his profound, melodic voice, and it caused

shudders to run down my spine. It had taken me off

monitor, so I totally disregarded the outstretched hand in

front of me.

"Sufficiently josie's," I said all things considered, still fairly stupefied,

pulling back from Louis. He lifted his temple and let his

arm tumble aside, his computing look meeting my

cut off one. Thus the abnormal quiet came to pass for us.

I made a sound as if to speak in a feeble endeavor to ease up the

temperament. I speculated I shouldn't exactly be unkind to the person

who had some way or another brought back my past sibling. So I

said the dumbest thing I could gather, "Erm... I've

heard you're an expert at skipping stones."

Indeed, smooth. I intellectually face-palmed myself, feeling

Louis' mercury eyes chuckling at me.

"I know a stunt or two I could show you," he gave,

winking at me. I was unable to help a blush that again crawled

all over at the allusion, however - believe it or not - I

had stepped on that trap myself. Well, since when did I

turn out to be so off-kilter with the young men?

I chose to disregard Louis' suggestion by and large.

My sibling had an alternate thought, though, completely neglectful of

the inference behind that one sentence... "That is perfect! Jo,

you should say OK! Might we at any point go at this point? Kindly, please,

pleaseee..."

"Perhaps later," I addressed reservedly. "We need to

go at this point. Mikey, express bye to your companion."

My sibling gave me a confounded look.

"However, why? I was by and large great! I sat idle. Louis,

tell her!" He went to a more interesting, upset, his eyes

glimmering as the monster looked through them.

I swallowed, unexpectedly restless. I needed to take Mikey to our

room before he would turn out to be considerably angrier and do

something unexplainable before the outsider - like

lift the vehicle or develop teeth and nails.

As I was going to mediate, Rosalynd's nephew tossed

me a fast, curious look, and he hunched before

Mikey, putting his lower arms kneeling down with the goal that his

hands were hanging unreservedly over the ground.

"Sure you were great, the best really," he relieved with

a grin, unsettling my sibling's wild hair. "In any case, your sister

needs you. What's more, we need to deal with our sisters,

right?" he added, peculiarly serious, and Mikey gestured,

reflecting Louis. I scrunched my temples in disarray,

feeling there was something else to the trade besides met the eye. What's more, unusually, my sibling knew precisely

what. It didn't agree with me. The entire effing

circumstance was past strange.

"Great," Louis mumbled, grinning at the seven-year-old.

"Listen for a minute, I'll come by tomorrow, and we'll take

Josie to the lake, and we'll show her how to skip stones. What is your take?"

Mikey's demeanor was precious, and it quieted the

storm that had gone off inside me after hearing

"Might we at any point go now?" My sibling asked, ideally.

"Apologies, Mikey. I actually need to wrap up with the vehicle, and afterward

I need to help my da."

"In any case, you guarantee we'll go tomorrow?" Mikey demanded.

"Scout guarantee."

I feigned exacerbation at that.

"Indeed, see you tomorrow then," my sibling moaned,

at long last yielding. "Bye, Louis."

"Bye, Mikey." I took my sibling's hand and directed him

towards the cabin. "See you tomorrow, Josie."

Definitely, makes no difference either way.

Chapter 5

"I'm. Not. Going. To. BED!!!" Roared Mikey, jumping at the dark brown leather couch and baring his teeth at our mum in an animalistic manner. It was almost 11 pm.

Mikey should have been asleep long ago, but we all got engrossed in a movie and lost track of time. And now that mum wanted to urge my brother to sleep, he was throwing a fit. "Mikey, we had a deal," Mum started patiently.

"The film ends, and you're going to bed. You know we have to get up early tomorrow.

We're going to Dover Hill." She added, still trying to reason with the kid, though I could clearly see it was a lost cause. Especially now that my brother decided to go apeshit.

"No! We're not going anywhere!"

He hollered, successfully waking up the whole house. Fortunately, we were alone in the lodge.

Rosalynd had gone to a family gathering or something, and no one else seemed to be actually staying in beside us, despite what she had told me the day before.

"Mikey!" Now, mum was shouting, helplessness tainting her voice.

I used my brother's distraction and sneaked behind him, trying to catch him off guard and take him off the couch, however, he somehow sensed me and slipped away from my grasp at an abnormal speed, leaving me perplexed.

He then abruptly turned around and looked at me with his eerily glowing eyes - his face contorted in a grotesque grimace, his canine teeth weirdly elongated.

Somewhere next to me, mum gasped and covered her mouth with her hand, her lips parted in a soundless scream.

Meanwhile, Mikey bared his teeth and leapt at me.

He took me completely by surprise.

I stumbled back, feeling his canines biting into my arm and breaking my skin.

I yipped, smelling blood, but before I could react in any way, Mikey jumped down from the couch and landed next to mum on all fours.

He then stood upright, shoved her out of his way, and rushed towards the outside doors.

The woman, still somewhat stupified, tripped on her feet and fell heavily on her backside.

I cursed loudly, rushing to help her up, just as I heard the front doors slamming shut.

"Quick, before we lose him!"

 She exclaimed, taking my hand.

We ran onto the front porch into the darkness and nagging cold. The wind almost immediately tugged at my hair, pulled some strands from my loose ponytail, and flung them in my face, bringing the smell of decayed leaves and dampness to my nose.

I let my eyes wander.

Mikey was nowhere in sight.

 "Mikey!" Mum called as she ran down the steps onto the gravel driveway. She whirled around, scrutinizing the darkness surrounding us, trying to see something through the dense undergrowth.

She couldn't, she wouldn't.

 "Mikey!"

I joined her, placing my hands on both sides of my mouth.

"Mikey, stop joking around! We get it! Mum and I won't force you to bed! Just... come out, please!"

"We're not angry, sweety!"

Mum took up after me.

"Come, we'll watch another movie! Maybe about the boy and his horse, the one you like so much?"

met with silence. Either my brother didn't hear us, or he was so agitated he didn't want to leave his hideout. "Mikey! Mikey, please, come out! This is not funny!"

Mum called out once more, getting desperate.

"Mikey!" I tried as well, again, to no avail.

I nervously brushed away the stray lock that fell on my face and bit my lip, distressed.

I had quite enough of constant tension, my brother's fits, and mum's fear.

I just wanted for everything to return back to normal when dad was still with us, and we didn't have to wander through cheap motels, hospitals, or chase after my crazed brother in the middle of the night at some Podunk. Back then, we had shot cans with an airgun and organized family board games night.

I had my friends.

I had my dad... I wanted my life back.

I felt my eyes prickle with tears. Just as I was about to finally lose it and break down in the middle of the driveway, the wind picked up... and carried Mikey's scent right to my nose.

My head snapped in the direction it came from.

Without thinking, I rushed towards the bushes.

Before I could be swallowed by the forest, though, mum clasped my arm, stopping me in the middle of my hunt. Strangely irritated,

I whirled on my heel and wrenched myself free, narrowing my gaze on her. I heard a low growl.

Mum immediately paled and stepped away, watching me with wide eyes.

She put her hands up as if she wanted to placate me or shield herself from me.

Me. Her daughter.

I felt as if I had been slapped.

The growling stopped while I blinked a couple of times to chase away a red that, at some point, tainted my vision.

I shook my head, clearing it, and mum winced.

She thought I was going to attack her. Oh, God. I froze, not knowing what to do. It was happening. I was becoming a monster. Mum was afraid of me.

I gulped, looking away from her, ashamed.

 "I think I know which way Mikey went,"

I mumbled through a clenched throat, breaking up the tense silence and fishing out my phone to distract myself.

 I turned on the torch. It illuminated the greyish tips of my once pristine trainers.

"I'll go after him. He must be scared."

 "You can't go alone," Mum suddenly said, licking her lips.

She made no move to touch me this time.

 Instead, she put her hands in the back pockets of her jeans, trying to hide how they trembled. "The forest is dangerous.

We don't know what animals are lurking in.

What if you get lost as well?"

 "We can't leave Mikey there, and one of us must be present... You know, in case he comes back,"

 I tried to be reasonable. "Besides... I know which way he had gone. I-I can s-smell him,"

 I stuttered, weakly. It was the first time I had mentioned the changes my body had started to undergo.

It was a taboo between me and mum. As long as we didn't talk about it, we could pretend I was normal.

It was Mikey, who was clearly changing.

He was the one who mentioned scents, and noises and showed weird, animalistic behaviours.

Not me

. I was pretty much normal, even though the doctors called my healing miraculous and wanted to run more tests on me before mum firmly refused. But I never mentioned any of the weird stuff.

 Mum brushed her hair at the back of her head, jittery. She had done it quite a lot lately.

A nervous habit of hers.

"Yeah, right...

 You can smell his scent. Yeah..." She mumbled, trying and failing to hide how much that one sentence had affected her.

 I used her distraction, unable to stand the way she was acting around me. Before mum could protest any further,

I let myself be swallowed by the bushes.

 I heard her calling out after me. She didn't follow

Chapter 6

We never saw it coming.

Dad's attack was as unexpected as finding out that what you believed to be a myth was, in fact, very real.

Werewolves existed.

But even now, after all that had happened,

 it sounded ridiculous to my ears. The funny thing was,

I didn't think about it all as I stumbled through the dense undergrowth, every now and then walking in the twigs that tugged on my already loose ponytail, tangling my hair and painfully ripping more strands from the tie and my skull.

 I was whipped on my face more than I could count whenever I wasn't careful enough. And I pretty much wasn't.

With how the moon hid behind thick, heavy clouds, the forest was shrouded in pitch darkness.

And while I had a torch on my phone and new night vision skills, they weren't enough to help me penetrate the blackness that had blanketed me the moment I had stepped my foot into the woods.

 I should have listened to my mum and stayed.

 I was glad I didn't. I could only imagine what my seven-year-old brother would feel when his rage finally subsided; when he would find himself lost and alone.

 So I pushed, despite the chills the creepy forest was giving me, trying hard not to think about the dangers lurking in the shadows.

Nope, I was most definitely not thinking about that at this particular moment. Ironically, it was then that some stupid bird decided to take off from a nearby tree.

 It jumped at me, fluttering its broad, dark wings, nearly hitting my head and almost giving me a heart attack.

I yelped, smacking the air around me, shooing the thing away as my heart threatened to fail.

 Effing birds and their effing ideas. I exhaled softly, brushing my hair at the back of my head with a trembling hand... only to hear a twig snap somewhere unnervingly close on my left. Still spooked from my previous unexpected encounter with mother nature, I whirled on my heel as a cold shiver once again ran down my spine.

"Mikey?"

 I asked, my voice hesitant.

I pointed the phone in the general direction of the creepy sound.

No one answered, nothing was there.

I shook my head, mad at my own cowardice. I had to chill, or I was sure to scare myself to death. And soon.

I turned around and picked up on Mikey's trail again - the soft, childish scent tainted by a sour tang of anger - lingering in the air.

It was like an arrow pointing me to the boy.

All I had to do, was follow.

Which I did, or at least wanted to, when I stepped on the loose stone, painfully twisting my ankle. I yipped, falling over.

Suddenly, I found myself rolling down the slope that miraculously appeared hell knew out of where.

The world started spinning around me as little pebbles dug in my skin, small sticks grazed my face, poking me through the hoodie, and dirt, mud, and bits of dead leaves landed on my tongue.

Thank God, I stopped as abruptly as I fell, ending up on the soft grass, spitting the dirt from my mouth while the clouded sky pivoted above me.

I blinked a couple of times, trying to get rid of dizziness, and propped myself on my elbows.

I was in a meadow of sorts surrounded by dark shades of slender trees that tried to grab the sky with their leave-less fingers.

Well, great. Tired of sitting on the cold, damp grass, I tried to stand up but the pain shot up from my left ankle.

I hissed and immediately grabbed the hurt area, feeling the heat radiating off it. If I was to guess, my ankle was most probably twisted. Just what I needed. Mumbling curses under my breath,

I turned on all fours in order to push myself to the standing position... And that was when

I heard a guttural growl.

My head snapped up, and my eyes collided with two icyblue orbs.

I gulped, somehow finding myself face to face with an enormous, light gray wolf.

It had its head lowered to the ground and ears glued to its sides as it flashed me with the row of its very sharp teeth, spit falling densely on the ground.

I felt the blood whooshing in my ears as the adrenaline kicked in.

I was a toast. [*] Once again, Louis Everton found himself looking for a tourist in the Redforest state park - and at nearly 12 fucking am, at that.

The funny thing was that - for the first time in his entire life - he actually hadn't minded being ripped away from what had possibly been the middle of the best afterparty Redforest had yet to witness.

Though truthfully, when his da had called, Louis had been pissed. At first, at least.

But, the second he had heard who the little lost sheep was,

Louis' legs moved as if of their own accord.

And thus, he was currently pacing the woods with a torch in his hand, uselessly dangling at his side.

He didn't need the artificial light to see in the dark - all thanks to his wolf's keen night vision skills - but the torch was there for the human's benefit and to 'keep up the appearances'. Or so his da insisted...

Tracing Josie wasn't hard for Louis, the best tracker or not.

The trail was easy to follow, and it was pretty much obvious the girl had no idea how to move about the forest, which bothered him more than he was ready to admit.

Well, even if Josie's movements weren't so apparent, Louis was sure her spicy, citrus aroma mixed with the light coppery tint of blood would tell him precisely where he had to head.

And so he trotted, soundlessly, with werewolf speed and grace, reaching the slope just as fucking Max Stone emerged on the other side of the meadow in his wolf form.

The twat had the decency to growl at the (not-so-human after all) girl.

Louis smelled her fear as it wafted to his nose, unexpectedly pissing his wolf off.

He couldn't help a low rumble that followed, which, on the other hand, drew Max's attention to him. Good.

The wolf's ears twitched as Max looked up - his watery eyes meeting Louis' quicksilver ones in a challenge. No surprises there

. Louis lifted his brow, staring the other boy down to show him who was at the top of the food chain, urging the annoying prick to just scram. They both knew Max couldn't handle Louis' wolf once he let him peek through his eyes. Maybe Louis would finally put the twat in his place once and for all...

If he would feel like it. Max finally backed down, nervously licking his nose and throwing Louis the last hateful glance before he skittered away. The idiot... [*]

The wolf's growling stopped as suddenly as it started.

The beast licked its nose in a - from what little I knew about dogs - submissive manner, and just like that, it leapt away, leaving me perplexed.

If that wasn't just weird... "Josie!" A familiar voice made me turn around as a warm, yellow light of a giant torch flooded me.

I placed my hand in front of my eyes, shading them, watching Louis swiftly and gracefully treading down the slope.

He was clad in a dark green windproof jacket, plain jeans, and converse sneakers. "Oh, thank God," I said, relieved.

"What are you doing here? How did you find me?" I asked, somewhat shocked.

"Auntie Rosie bumped into your mum when she was on her way from a family meeting,"

Louis explained, nearing me. His smell - a mixture of sandalwood, rain, sweat, and musk, totally suppressed by the scent of oil and car waste earlier before - wafted to my nose, making me all jittery and funny as a result.

I gulped, leaning away while his quicksilver eyes looked me up and down, stopping on my left leg, still awkwardly suspended in the air.

"Can you walk?" He asked, concerned, nodding at my ankle.

"I'm good," I shrugged, trying to put some weight on my foot. The stabbing prickles immediately followed, making me wince from pain. "Or maybe not...

I think I need your help," I bit my lip, feeling my cheeks turn pink from embarrassment.

"I have to find Mikey. He ran into the woods and probably got lost.

He must be scared..." "My dad's on it. He will find him in no time.

He knows these woods like the back of his hand. C'mon, let me take you to the lodge.

Your mum's beyond herself. She's somewhat broken down on Rosalynd," he said, giving me his back as he crouched in front of me.

I sighed, nervously rubbing my face with my hands, suddenly tired of everything. I didn't know what to do anymore, whom to help - my lost brother or unstable mother. Louis seemed to sense my dilemma as he inclined his head, eyeing me from the side.

"Easy, Josie. We have loads of tourists getting lost in the forest every year, and my dad has tracked and found every single one of them and brought them home.

If it makes you feel better, though,

I can help da out after I drop you at the lodge," he assured me and then waved at me with his hand.

"C'mon, hop on, I really don't bite. That is, unless you ask..."

I actually barked out a laugh at his lame joke, surprising myself.

"Do the girls seriously fall for that?"" I asked, conceding. "All the time,"

he grinned without missing a beat. Shaking my head, I finally placed my hands on his arms and wrapped my left, then right leg around his torso.

He lifted me as if I weighed nothing, his scent wrapping me like a cozy blanket, soothing me.

It was strange how the guy I bearly knew made me ease up so quickly.

I hadn't felt so light-hearted in the whole effing week. "Let me call my da first, so he knows you're with me,"

Louis said, giving me a torch. He fished for his phone and dialed the correct number.

"It's Louis," I heard him murmur after a second beep, his tone oddly business-like.

"Yeah, I've got her... There was a little... incident, but she's fine...

Can't really talk right now. Great, okay.

We'll meet you up at Rosie's... I know..." "Has your dad found Mikey?"

I asked the minute he hung up.

"Yep. He's okay. They are on their way to the lodge.

We'll meet up there," he answered, and I breathed a sigh of relief. Louis started to walk up the slope.

"Mind telling me why did your brother run for the woods in the first place?"

I sighed.

"It's a long story." "Well, try me."

I had no idea why, but I did.

Chapter 7

Our walk was unexpectedly quick.

It was clear Louis was familiar with the forest.

He could have walked in blindsided and still found his way home.

His steps were sure and unusually quiet as he moved around dead leaves and twigs thickly littering the floor, never placing his foot on the wrong spot.

The only sound I could hear was his soft even breathing, which apparently had a strangely therapeutic effect on my shattered nerves.

I felt so relaxed and, well, safe despite him being a total stranger that I almost fell asleep on his back.

I even found myself leaning my forehead against the nook of his neck at one point - to my utmost embarrassment.

Not that Louis minded.

The closer we got to the house, however, the darker my mood became until we hit the gravel path and, once again, anxiety twisted my insides.

"You alright there?"

Louis asked suddenly, his melodic voice lulling some of my panic. "Y-Yeah... All's good,"

I lied, trying to sound sure where, in fact,

I was far from it. I dreaded meeting with mum after my little outburst.

I was afraid of the look on her face, terrified to learn that she would still be scared of me, that she would reject me.

Louis didn't comment on my lie, though it took no genius to tell he didn't buy the word I said.

Not when he could feel my iron-like grip on his shoulders.

"Your mum must be worried,"

he murmured, correctly guessing where my thoughts drifted, and I willed myself to relax.

We covered those four-five steps leading to the porch and neared the doors in no time.

My pulse picked up, and my heart started hammering in my chest, threatening to break out of my rib cage.

 Louis went inside the lodge and into a corridor.

The warmth immediately hugged my chilled body, but I felt nothing but the jumbled nerves that were gnarling my insides and driving me crazy with stress.

We headed straight for the spacious, rustic style kitchen from where mum's and Rosalynd's voices were drifting.

 Once inside, I carefully slid down Louis' back, closing my eyes as I braced myself for rejectionWhich never came.

 "Josie, thank God!" I heard instead as the quick steps followed.

Mum wrapped me in her warm embrace, squeezing me so hard as if she was scared I would suddenly perish in front of her.

 Warm tears prickled my eyes, and I hugged mum back, smelling her familiar, motherly scent and finally falling apart in her grasp.

"I'm sorry,"

 I whispered softly, though I wasn't even sure for what was I apologising. It didn't mind - mum understood. "Shh, it's not your fault.

 It's alright, it's okay, sweety.

I've got you, I've got you..."

She murmured softly into the side of my head, her voice clogged as she stroked my tumbled hair while I sobbed silently.

"Let me make some tea," Rosalynd suddenly decided. "Jack is probably on his way with Mikey as we speak."

I sniffed, finally collecting myself and unglueing from mum, red rushing down my face to my neck as I quickly wiped the tears from my cheeks.

Out of the corner of my eye,

I spotted Louis.

He was leaning against the wall with his arms crossed over his chest and one leg propped on the hard surface behind him.

His attention was solely on the ground, and he didn't look up, even though I could tell he felt my gaze...

I gulped, biting my lip as I shifted my attention back to Rosalynd, unable to stand the vibes I was getting from the boy.

I understood on some primal level that he was thoroughly pissed, though nothing, absolutely nothing, indicated it.

My eyes landed on Rosalynd, who was still wearing a burgundy, floor-length dress from the party.

It wrapped around her legs as she made her way to the big, wooden table standing in the middle of the kitchen.

She looked royal, like a queen, but still somehow motherly with the cups of steaming tea in both her hands.

"Louis, stop standing there like an idiot, drilling a hole in my floor, and sit down,"

She chid her nephew, drawing his attention.

The boy snapped out of whatever dark place he had been, and a crooked smile curved the side of his mouth.

It didn't reach his eyes.

"Nah, I'm good," he said when the front doors opened. I smelled my brother before his childish voice reached my ears.

"Mikey..." I whispered, turning around just as the boy rushed into the kitchen and straight in my arms.

"Josie!"

He screamed excitedly as I lifted him off the ground, hugging him tightly. "Never run off like that again, you silly-billy,"

I breathed into his hair, taking comfort in his smell.

Then, the strangest thing happened.

"You!" Exclaimed mum accusingly as a man I had never seen in my life appeared in the doorframe.

I looked at him, noticing how tall he was with his 6′8".

Just like Louis, he had jet black hair (although his was closely cropped to his skull), quicksilver irises, strong jaw, and lean silhouette, concealed by the thick, woolen turtleneck and unzipped navy-blue jacket he wore.

"That is surely an unexpected turn of today's events,"

The man, Jack, if I got that right, said calmly, raising his brows. "Do you know each other?"

Asked Rosalynd curiously, just as mum suddenly grabbed her from behind and locked her elbow around the woman's throat in a choking manner, holding a knife she had pulled literally out of nowhere to her neck, a stone-cold expression on her face.

"Mum, what is going on?" I loudly demanded while a guttural growl vibrated through the room, and Louis took a step forward.

As if on que, Jack's large hand landed on his son's shoulder, stopping him.

Mikey started to shake in my hold. "The blade is silver.

Take another step, and I swear I will shove it straight in her neck," mum said in an odd voice while she tightened her hold around Rosalynd's throat. "Easy, Melinda,"

Jack directed his words at my mum, but it was Louis, who reluctantly relaxed under his dad's hold.

"What does it even matter, mum? And why the heck are you holding a knife to Rosalynd's neck?" I cut in, my voice incredulous and strangely loud in my ears.

I licked my suddenly chapped lips, tension making me sick to my stomach.

Mum ignored me.

"Josephine, go upstairs and bring our luggage down. Take your brother with you."

"But mum..."

"Do as I say!" She screamed at me, and I winced while Mikey started to cry.

"I thank you for your hospitality and finding my son, Jack.

We're leaving, and if you let us go in peace nobody will get hurt."

"You're making a mistake," The man's voice was calm as he regarded mum cooly.

"There is no cure for what your children are going through.

It can't be stopped and you know that. Dover Hill is all a rouse. Your so called friends lied to you to lure you in. They will take your kids from you and use them like lab rats.

And after they'll be done torturing them, they will get rid of them," he said as a matter of fact, nodding ever so slightly at Rosalynd, who answered him in the same way.

Mum didn't see it, too distracted by her own frenzy.

"Shut up. Shut up! You know nothing!" She exclaimed, loosening her grip on Rosalynd's throat.

"It's because of your kind that my family...!"

Quicker than a flash, Louis' aunt somehow slipped from mum's grasp, spun on her heel, and knocked mum cold with the side of her hand.

I gasped as mum's eyes closed shut, and she fell straight in the Rosalynd's outstretched arms. Mikey stopped crying while I gaped like a fish to the silence that followed.

Chapter 8

"Louis, take Mrs. Hart to the indignation the executives room,"

Jack's structure shocked me out of anything that daze I had sunk

in.

"What? No!" I terrified as my eyes snapped to Louis'

father. He dealt with my look, not avoiding the

stacked look I gave him. It was the main sign the

man heard me and recognized my complaints. A

benevolence of sorts.

"Josie, it's alright," Rosalynd ringed in delicately, attempting to

ease me however achieving the specific inverse.

"No, it's not alright. Nothing is alright! My mum held a blade

to your neck, and you don't for even a moment appear to be staged, and

presently... Presently you are taking her to a room that sounds

terribly a great deal like prison! Shouldn't something be said about it, do implore tell, is

OK?!" I yelled, hurling boisterously.

My little eruption failed to attract anyone's attention. Louis didn't even

spare me a look as he followed with whatever his father

had requested him to do, his appearance shut. I bit my

lip, feeling the harsh taste of treachery on my tongue

(however I didn't actually have the foggiest idea why I felt double-crossed by the

kid I scarcely knew in any case) while he cautiously

took mum from Rosalynd's arms and supported her to his

chest.

"Where are you taking her? Where are you taking my

mum?!" I requested, venturing forward to stop Louis.

Tragically, my lower leg picked that second to remind

me it was as yet harmed. The aggravation punctured my foot as I

stumbled aside, murmuring softly. I moved

the heaviness of my body, changing Mikey in my hold. His

poundage positively wasn't turning out to be useful to the harmed

region, yet I tried not let him out of my arms.

Not with those individuals around.

"It's simply a room in a storm cellar, Josie, nothing to stress

about," Rosalynd at long last made sense of, tossing Jack a look

I was unable to unravel.

"It doesn't seem don't like anything," I countered, my voice

dribbling with mockery while I disregarded the pair's quiet

discussion. Mikey embraced me closer, concealing his face

in the hooligan of my neck as he cried delicately, shaking.

He was fomented, and it annoyed me such a lot of I was

getting frantic to ease him. I made a mitigating commotion at

the rear of my throat, delicately running my hand up and

down his back in a quieting way.

"Could someone at any point let me know what is happening?" I asked once more,

baffled.

"How have you been turned?" Jack out of nowhere chosen to

elegance me with his consideration, however not the way I

expected.

I flickered, fixing my hang on Mikey as I expressed, "I'm

not certain what no doubt about it."

Lie.

Jack didn't try to remark on it, giving me a

pointed look as he gestured for me to take a seat at the

table. I hesitantly followed, setting Mikey in my lap

while the man took the seat inverse me. Rosalynd

moved the cups of tea before us, however she didn't join

us at the table, resting up against the counter all things considered. I

snatched the cup she offered and pulled it closer,

smelling a sickish fragrance of melissa. It made my

stomach stir.

"Allow me to reword the inquiry: who has torn into you,

Josie? Reality, kindly," Jack thundered gradually, his

mercury eyes checking my response as he bound his

hands on the table and inclined forward.

I promptly stepped back, abruptly wrecked.

The perspiration broke over my upper lip and on the scruff of

my neck, my unfortunate response simply natural. Some

a piece of me knew who the greater hunter was - the red

ready lights cried the caution in my cerebrum, and I felt a
shudder run down my spine. Notwithstanding that, I opened my
mouth to ramble a falsehood, yet Mikey beat me to the punch.
"It was our dad," He provided, his voice shy as he
inhaled into the side of my neck. "Our dad transformed into a
colossal awful wolf, and he nibbled us."
[*]
The appearance of dissatisfaction and double-crossing composed on
Josie's face tormented Louis while he conveyed Mrs. Hart
down the stairs to the outrage the executives room.
Albeit the kid knew the discipline his father forced
on the individual for going after the Luna of the Pack was
ridiculously indulgent, his wolf actually battled Louis for
control, prepared to challenge their Alpha; prepared to
challenge their own dad - the main man whose
judgment they totally trusted. What's more, why? Since
the young lady Louis scarcely knew felt hurt.
The kid was confounded.
He pushed the steel entryways with his hip as he strolled
inside the room he had invested such a lot of energy in when he
was a little guy.
Louis wasn't generally in line with his wolf. The two of them
had an attitude, and even now, they in some cases battled
with controling their resentment. Most predominant guys did
Also, prevailing Louis was. He was additionally mateless,

seeing that there weren't however many conceived females as

guys, and those turned barely endure their most memorable shift.
Werewolves' reality was basically overwhelmed by

dicks.

Which completely sucked in the event that anybody asked him.

Louis checked out the spot. His mercury eyes

skimmed over the paw denotes that harmed the thick

dull-dark substantial walls and halted at a solitary bed

solidly got to the floor - the main household item

inside. The simple like set helped him to remember a jail

cell yet, as Louis came to gain from his own

experience, there was a merciless common sense behind the

moderate plan. The less free things implied, the

less things would be tossed at the walls or tore to

pieces by seething wolves. It was basic like that. The

room was not really used to keep detainees in any case, so

there was no genuine requirement for convenience. Most frequently

than not, the adversaries of the Pack were managed on the

spot... with the uncommon exemptions of frenzied human

huntresses, evidently.

What's more, Josie's mum was only that - a huntress. The tattoo

Louis spotted behind her right ear told him so much. He

questioned Mrs. Hart had been extremely dynamic as of late,

Her reflexes had been too messy, in addition to her children

obviously had no clue about their mom's tomfoolery.

Any other way, Josie wouldn't be so blown a gasket by Melinda's little episode in the kitchen.

Louis breathed out delicately, tenderly laying the lady on the sleeping cushion, and he left, shutting the entryways behind him. He didn't lock them - there was compelling reason need. Mrs. Hart wouldn't get out regardless of whether she attempted, on the grounds that there wasn't

any handle inside. It was another action carried out to keep the unsound wolves in; one that evidently proved to be useful while managing huntresses, too.

Which carried Louis to the inquiry in question - how the damnation had they given a tracker access their nest in any case? Furthermore, what was the association between his da and Josie's mother? The Alpha had clearly perceived her from some place...

It hit Louis hard as he began to climb the steps and then strolled into the kitchen, just to hear Mikey say, "It was our dad. Our dad transformed into a gigantic terrible wolf, and he bit us."

Chapter 9

The real truth was formally out in the open.

I felt Rosalynd's and Jack's cryptic looks that told me

precisely nothing, and I gulped, feeling the blood

whooshing in my ears. I unexpectedly stood up, more than

prepared to cut off.

"Alright, little mate, it's sleep time for you," I chose,

attempting to cover for Mikey, who had only fessed up to

anything that Louis' dad was suggesting. Something the

reasonable piece of my cerebrum was all the while attempting to deny. Also,

hard.

In any case, I was excessively drained for this poo. Too drained to even
consider sharing

my family's soil with the outsiders I didn't know anything

about and whom I scarcely trusted. Particularly after the

stunt, they had pulled on my mum. Additionally, it was cracking

12 PM.

I met Rosalynd's golden eyes, seeing trouble in them,

and afterward moved my look back to Jack. His face was still

incomprehensible to me as he rested back up against the seat

furthermore, folded his arms over his chest, his muscles protruding

under the dim sweater.

"We'll talk in the first part of the day then," he concurred gradually later
a delay, in regards to me cooly. I wriggled under his
choking out gaze, attempting to seem more valiant than I was.
Tragically, we both realized I was tricking no one with
my unfortunate demonstration. Say thanks to God, I was out of the blue saved
by Louis, who unexpectedly arose out of the lobby.
"I'll show the kin back to their room then," He
offered, causing Jack to notice himself. My
contracted lungs loose, and I believed I could at long last
relax. I breathed in cool sweet air through my nose.
Smooth Josie, genuine smooth.
"Great. You know the drill," Jack gestured as the kid
moved toward me, holding out his outstretched arms to
take my sibling. I pulled back right away, feeling
agonizing feeling when I set my foot in some unacceptable position.
It hurt like bitch, however I uttered no sound. I was a long way from
showing any more shortcoming before the three.
Louis' temples wrinkled, and he murmured delicately. "Here we go,
Josie, I won't hurt your sibling. I simply need to
assist you with conveying him higher up."
"What's more, you believe that I should accept that after you've quite recently taken
my mum to some obscure cellar room?" I gritted out,
giving him the evil eye.
He snarled right in front of him, running his hand through
his dark black hair in irritation.

"Fine, do what you need," He at long last piece back, his eyes
abandoning mercury to light dark, shocking me.
"Yet, don't think twice about it later. Presently, come."
In spite of the fact that I was a long way from cheerful about being requested
around, my feet moved willingly, something
in me provoking me to follow. I gulped the delicate
groan that burst all the rage when one more rush of agony
struck me for the umpteenth time this evening.
This was going downhill exceptionally quick.
We left the kitchen - me toward the front, Louis hot on my
heels - and I set out toward the steps. I attempted to cajole Mikey
down once before the initial step, however my younger sibling
wouldn't have it. I could coarseness my teeth at that and
continue to gradually ascend, perspiring and puffing from
the work this little action caused me. I felt Louis' look
boring an opening at the rear of my head the whole time,
his baffled fits blending in with my own depleted
ones. Notwithstanding that, I didn't ask him for help, and he
didn't offer once more, despite the fact that I had this odd inclination he
truly needed to.
I at last arrived at the arrival and halted unexpectedly,
holding the railing like a help as the high contrast
spots detonated before my eyes. My temple, armpits,
furthermore, back were doused in sweat, and I was shy of
breath. What was more terrible, I was additionally genuinely certain my
lower leg

could take nothing else of the moving with the extra
weight.
Indeed, crap.
"What will happen to us? What will occur
to my mum?" I asked in a frantic endeavor to occupy
myself from contemplating going through the
second piece of what immediately turned into my own
limbo.
I wouldn't arrive at the second floor with Mikey in my
hold. It was absolutely impossible that I could do that.
I licked my dried out lips, getting Louis' warmed gaze in
my fringe vision.
I went to confront him, shocked to see his eyes were
on fire with repressed outrage, his hands jerking at his
sides as he held them set up with seemingly a
incredible trouble.
"It depends," Was all he replied, and my disappointment
sped up.
"On what?" I gritted out.
"On your mom." Louis deadpanned. "...And my father.
Yet, do you truly need to have that discussion now, with your
sibling tuning in? He is adequately terrified."
It stunned me Louis had seen that by any stretch of the imagination. I moreover
couldn't contend with his thinking, so I moaned, stopping
fire for the present. There went my redirection, eh. I gazed toward

one more stairway, giving it a last sad look

before I prepared myself for some more aggravation. Prior to I

made another stride, however, I heard a delicate, "Josie, let me

help you." Followed by somewhat more frantic, "Please."

I turned my head to the side intersection my eyes with

Louis' hysterical ones. I was not prepared to concede rout, yet I

was likewise almost certain I wouldn't arrive at the top with my

pride alone. I wanted the kid's effing help, whether I

enjoyed it, or not.

Louis probably seen the second's shortcoming on my

face as he burned through no time strolling nearer and delicately

lifting Mikey from my arms. Hesitantly I let him, my

beating, depleted lower leg inviting a short reprieve. I

nearly shouted out of help.

Mikey, being the little swindler he was, right away

loosened up in's serious areas of strength for Louis, and I shook my head.

I then began to climb the steps once more, driving our little

gathering of three to my and Mikey's transitory room - a

fancier rendition of what certainly was currently our jail

cell.

* * *

I was surprised conscious by a hand tenderly shaking my

shoulder. I pivoted, my languid look floating

towards a natural sets of naval force blue eyes.

"Mum?" I asked distrustfully, promptly sitting up

also, watching her put her pointing finger all the rage,

motioning for me to stay calm.

"Shh. Mikey's still sleeping," She murmured. I looked at

my sibling, spread next to me like a starfish. His

chest ascended and down as delicate wheezes left his halfopened mouth. He was unconscious, which wasn't

amazing as it was as yet dim outside. I didn't know whether I

had even two hours' rest.

I painstakingly slid up and followed mum outside. I

couldn't resist the opportunity to see she was wearing unique

garments that she had worn when she had been taken to

the indignation the executives room. It likewise appeared to be that she

had as of late had a shower. Her inexactly hitched

earthy colored hair was as yet soggy, and she possessed an aroma like cleanser and

peach-scented cleanser.

Mum rapidly and discreetly drove me ground floor, her means

light on a wooden floor. I trailed behind her, actually trying

to sort out what was happening and why she woke me

up around midnight. How could she escape this

odd room?

I was so restless toward the finish of our little round of sneaking

around that I didn't understand I wasn't limping

any longer - my foot should have completely recuperated while I rested. We arrived at the primary arrival, and I spotted Louis

resting up against the wall at the lower part of the steps. I

scowled, again considering what was happening, as my
look moved to Jack remaining close to Louis. Blood
depleted from my face.

"Mum, care to make sense of what's truly going on with this?" I inquired
gradually, as we bet everything and the kitchen sink step and regarded
ourselves as next
to the two. An unexpected sensation of fear turned my
internal parts.

Mum unexpectedly changed direction suddenly, and she pulled me
towards her, making me stagger. I slammed into her
body with a delicate snort, yet she disregarded it. She began
murmuring in my ear, her words hysterical. "Pay attention to me
Josie, and you listen well. Those individuals, there are right here
very much like you and Mikey, they are werewolves, and they
will assist you with going through your most memorable progress."

"W-What? What are you referring to? W-What about
the cure...?" I squirmed away from her hold. I was absolutely
confounded. "You guaranteed you would help us! You said
there were specialists at Dover Hill who could forestall us
from transforming into... into m-beasts... You've said it
yourself!"

"There is no fix!" Mum cut me off, grasping my
shoulders and shaking me, her voice loaded with despair.

"Individuals I believed as long as I can remember steered me off track! They
utilized me. They simply needed to... Goodness my God..." Mum
shut her eyes, as she covered her mouth with her

hand, attempting to gather herself. I looked at Louis and
Jack. Their looks were inauspicious, Louis' miserable even...
Mum breathed out boisterously, like she was attempting to support
herself. I snapped my consideration back to her. "Jack and
his Pack... They will help you, Josie. They will help both
you and Mikey endure the shift... They will instruct you
instructions to control the monster, so it won't hurt anybody. In any case
you need to remain. You need to remain, and I can't. I c-can't. I
need to leave..."
She didn't appear to be legit. Mum look bad to
me. Had she at last lost every one of her marbles in the storm cellar
room?
"No, no, no, no, no, no. This is totally off base. You're not my
mum. My mom, Melinda Hart, wouldn't simply leave her
messes with complete outsiders! What have they done to
you?" I asked, stunned, my words delicate even to my ears.
"How have you treated my mom?!" I thundered as a
white-hot burst of outrage filled my veins. I jumped at the
first individual next to me, pushing mum out of my way, my
hands molded like paws, lips twisted back in a horrendous
growl, prepared to eliminate the danger.
Louis had me stuck against his body before I could
indeed, even cause any genuine harm. My back hit his hard chest as
he locked his hands around me, mumbling alleviating
nothings in my hair.

"Let me go! Allow me fucking to go, you prick! Let me gooo..."
I cried, losing my force, falling on myself.
Hot tears were spilling down my face. "You can't
leave us, mum." My lower lip was wobbling and
everything was hazy. "Please..." I asked.
"I love you both, sweety," Mum chocked out. She, as well,
was crying. "I guarantee I'll return. Deal with your
sibling."
"No! Try not to go! You can't go! You can't!"
In any case, she left

Chapter 10

Birds peeped uproariously in the trees.
I was relaxed in the warm sun beams, and keeping in mind that their
delicate light stroked my uncovered skin, the breath that
left my mouth made little hazy puffs before my
face.
It was cold outside.
I was perched on the wooden seat on the yard, the cup
of now chilly tea long failed to remember in my grasp, and I was
gazing vacantly at the country road ahead that disappeared
some place in the trees right at the edge of the forest.
A similar street my mum required a couple of hours prior.
It seemed like a lifetime.
I actually didn't let Mikey know that mum had left us. For one's purposes, he

was right now dozing. It was wicked six in the

morning, all things considered, and two, I truly didn't have the foggiest idea what to

say. I couldn't simply dump the news on him like that...

I feared coming clean with him.

I murmured, inclining my head back with the goal that I was confronting the

wooden roof. It was difficult to accept how crappy

my life became in a range of seven days. My father transformed into

a beast, and we needed to crawl under a rock. Mum

deserted us, and we currently ended up at the

kindness of certain outsiders who professed to be werewolves. We had no place else to go except if I took a vehicle. What's more,

cash. I unexpectedly turned into a sole supplier of a seven-yearold kid at eighteen years old - and I wasn't prepared to do

it - so I needed to get a new line of work. Something fair and all day. I needed to become acclimated to the possibility that I would go fuzzy

pretty soon, and I could fail to address it in light of the fact that,

clearly, the fix didn't exist.

Sheesh, this most likely sucked.

I shut my still red and stinging eyes and sniffed my

watery nose. I wasn't crying. I quit doing that

part of the way during that time when the tears declined to

stream.

Light strides intruded on my solitary melancholy party. They

were trailed by the smell of chocolate and the particular

fragrance of lilac I previously perceived.

Rosalynd tracked down me - not that it was troublesome.

"Coca?" She asked positioning her head aside and

giving me a cup.

I looked at her through the lashes, then shrugged. I took

a cup and traded the virus drink for a hot one, at the same time,

once more, I didn't drink it. All things being equal, I inclined forward,

holding the cup between my spread legs, and looked

back at the forest while the lady rested close to me.

We sat peacefully briefly, paying attention to the

birds peeping.

"You realize your mom would have rather not left?" Rosalynd

begun, taking a taste of her beverage. Espresso, my nose

chosen.

"Mhm," I muttered, my voice dull.

The lady looked at me from the side with her golden

eyes. They were boring an opening in my mind, yet I didn't

respond. Following a little while, Rosalynd surrendered. She

murmured.

"Jack had no other decision. He needed to drive your mum

away. She went after me, the Luna of the Pack. Under

typical conditions, it generally implies demise on the

spot," she made sense of, however it actually didn't make any

sense. I had no clue about who that Luna was. In any case,

the assertion at last cajoled a response out of me.

"Killing individuals isn't a method for taking care of issues, you know?" I said, another inclination encouraging alive in my chest.

Outrage.

"It is on the planet you're presently living in. Most frequently,

As may be obvious, there are exemptions... Your

mum is one," Rosalynd countered smoothly.

"All things considered, simply fab! Furthermore, you maintain that I should do what happens next?

Praise Jack? He might have quite recently killed her; the

result would be something similar," I snarled. My breaths

were weighty and noisy, my hands fisted at my lap.

The lady's eyes flashed yellow and as before long returned

back to ordinary.

"No, it wouldn't, and that's what you know. Your mum can't

get back to the pack land because of reasons she impeccably

comprehends. I realize you love her, and your sentiments

may dazzle you to reality, yet your family isn't as

honest as you might naturally suspect. Your father wasn't nibbled for

not an obvious explanation. Melinda told us as much before she left."

"What are you in any event, referring to?" I asked angrily,

confronting Rosalynd and daggering her with my eyes.

She could have done without it - the low snarl that right away

followed told me so much. Yet, I disregarded it. I moreover

overlooked the annoying inclination, which provoked me to look

away. I didn't, despite the fact that disquiet attempted to supersede me,

slithering my internal parts crude.

Once more, rosalynd snarled, a piece stronger now, her golden eyes on fire, a monster looking through it. I snapped my

look away, and similarly as unexpectedly, this inclination inside me

died down. It annoyed me, and I grasped my clench hands

harder at my lap, my nails diving in the delicate skin of my

palms, drawing blood.

Rosalind moaned and shook her head.

"Your family ancestry isn't really for me to tell. Yet, you've

been a piece of this world longer than you might naturally suspect.

Your dad was an extremely skilled tracker all things considered," she

said after stopping for a moment.

I snapped my look back to her, my temples wrinkling.

"What's up with being a tracker?" I asked, attempting to

comprehend anything that she was inferring. I knew my

father used to go on end of the week trips with his companions to

lessen the number of inhabitants in a few creature animal categories. However, it

was finished inside unofficial laws. Nothing out

of the standard thing.

Rosalynd sneered, however her grin was harsh.

"It relies upon what you're hunting," she countered

obscurely. "However, that is a discussion for some other time. Presently, we have more

squeezing matters to examine. Most importantly, do you know

anything about werewolves?"

* * *

We were moved to the Alpha's home. Evidently, that

was what their chief, Jack, was called. The Alpha. I still
deep down jeered at whatever point I heard the term. It sounded
absurd.

The house seemed to be a little manor, in spite of the fact that it was
as a matter of fact a lodge with two carports and dim
tiles. It was found further into the forest and was
encircled by more modest cabin houses that sprung out of
the ground without a genuine plan or sense. It still
looked in some way arranged.

Jack was the main one to welcome us, however I could feel quite a large number
inquisitive eyes on me. Being in a spotlight as was that
worrying me, and I needed to drive myself not to squirm
or on the other hand wriggle. Nature let me know it would be deciphered as
shortcoming, and I was unable to be feeble with my sibling
under my consideration.

I pressed Mikey's hand harder and constrained myself to
try to avoid panicking while my sibling drew nearer to my legs,
wriggling next to me and obviously attempting to show up even
more modest than he previously was. He whimpered, incapable to
lift the heaviness of the undesirable notoriety, and began to smell
of dread and stress. My defense went into supersede.

Driven by nature, I protected my sibling with my body,
evening out my environmental elements with a deadly look as an
unnatural, throaty snarl out of the blue left my mouth.

The entire circumstance was vexing.

Jack at long last seen our disturbance and chose to give a
damn. I had no clue about what he did at the same time, abruptly, the looks
recently halted, and I could at long last inhale a bit.
The man - or rather a werewolf/the Alpha - grinned.
"The Pack can be a torment in some cases. We share an excessive number of
similitudes with our wolf cousins. What's more, as you can
obviously see, interest is one of such," Jack made sense of, not
precisely contritely, as he moved toward us, his moves
slow and purposely unharmful. I watched him like a
peddle the whole time, still not letting my watchman down
regardless of his endeavors to show up less undermining. He
disregarded my dubiousness and basically sat on his
hunches before Mikey and gave him a comforting grin.
He even set up his fisted hand so my sibling could
knock it in a hello.
"How goes it with you, minimal one?" He cooed, his voice
milder.
My sibling gave Jack a bashful fistbump. His fragrance gradually
gotten back to business as usual as he began to unwind, and it facilitated
my broke nerves accordingly.
"Is my Mommy in the house?" The kid asked hesitantly.
"Mum went out traveling, Munchkin. We've proactively talked
about it," I mumbled, scouring his arm soothingly.
"Your sister's right. Your mum needed to head off to some place,
what's more, you and Josie will remain with me for some time. Is

that OK?" Jack filled in without a hitch, his eyes flashing
with bitterness.
He might have tricked me.
Mikey positioned his head to the side like a canine.
"However, provided that you don't make Josie cross. I can't stand it when
she's cross," he chose, taking me totally unsuspecting.
I tossed him a shocked look while Jack giggled,
unsettling Mikey's mop of hair. "Smartass, ain't ya? I can't
guarantee I won't at any point disturb your sister, yet I'll attempt.
Okay?"
My sibling appeared to reflect on his words over.
This discussion was getting stranger and more peculiar.
"Okay..." He at long last concurred and similarly as unexpectedly different
the subject. "Is Louis with you? We could skip stones!"
Mikey confronted me with a hopeful look, and I made due
to give him a little, feeble grin.
"That we would be able," I conceded, then nearly bounced as a
natural, melodic voice dug out from a deficit me.
"Sounds great."
I whipped around to see Louis approaching us with a wide
bless his attractive face. He was dressed a piece like a
fighter - clad in all green with a little exemption for
dark freight boots that arrived at up to a portion of his calf. Louis'
hair was unsettled by the breeze, and he wore a light
sheen on his brow, as though he had recently been

running. His mercury eyes appeared to shimmer in the

sun beams.

A peculiar fluffy inclination pooled in the pits of my stomach

as my heart skirted a thump. I glared. Might it be said that i was a bonehead?

That person had deceived me two times in a single evening. I still

hadn't excused him for seizing my mum and

mauling me. For what reason would i say i was drawn to him? Was I

Rational?

"Louis!" Mikey shouted, slipping from my grip.

He raced to Louis - causing me a deep sense of disquiet - and the other

kid lifted Mikey and quickly put him on his

shoulders. My sibling giggled while I fisted my hands

at my sides. I was clashed. I couldn't say whether the entirety

picture in front mitigated me or disturbed. I could have done without that

Louis weaseled into Mikey's effortlessness so rapidly. Really I didn't

like it.

I could have done without that the slightest bit.

"All will resolve eventually," Jack abruptly said,

grinning at Louis' and Mikey's jokes. "I realize it doesn't

look it the present moment, yet it'll be okay. When you shift and

figure out how to control your wolf, I'll allow you to meet your

mum."

If Jack had any desire to pacify me, he had done a poo work.

"You'll let me?" I spat out.

Louis' father gave me a wide, ruthless smile.

"I'll let you." He rehashed, ruling out
conversation. "The present moment, you're a threat to yourself and
your environmental elements. You'll wind up battling for
control with your wolf to an ever increasing extent, however I'll help you
with that. We as a whole will. Furthermore, when you are prepared to leave,
you'll be allowed to go. Except if, obviously, you'll choose to
remain." He said, looking at me dead without flinching. I digit my lip
furthermore, thought of myself as gesturing. "Only one really hing,
Josephine. Try not to share your family subtleties with any of
the Pack. Basically not yet. How about we simply say there would be
some unpleasantries would it be advisable for anyone anybody learn you're
Melinda's girl."
I felt the blood channel from my face.
"Your meaning could be a little clearer."
Jack recently grinned.

Chapter 11

"Are you going hunting once more?" I ask father as I stroll into
the kitchen.

It is ten PM, and Mikey is now sleeping while mum
has rested off on the couch before the TV. Father and I
appear to be the main two physically functional. It happens very
frequently, truth be told. However, I don't care about it; I like my alone
In any case, time with father - for the most part.
Prior to his chases? Not really.

Father looks at me from behind the firearm he is cleaning
while I open the cooler and take out the squeezed orange. I sit
on one of the seats inverse father's as he stacks
the clasp with silver slugs. I take one in my grasp and
place it under the light, watching it reflect warm yellow
kitchen lights.

"What's with silver?" I ask, inquisitive while I put the shot
back on the table and push it with my finger. It starts to
turn with a trademark ringing sound. "Isn't it, as,
more yielding than the ordinary projectiles?"

Father gets the projectile and places it in the clasp in a quick,
polished move, evening out me with his green eyes as he
does. He generally wears the most peculiar articulations at whatever point

he is setting himself up for chases. His face appears to be cold and far off, so not the same as the typical warm and open one I'm utilized to. Also, he generally expresses the most abnormal things. "A few things can be put out just with silver. You recollect that well, Josephine."

* * *

"This is your new room," expressed Louis hauling me out of my memory.

I studied the room from my spot at the doorstep while Mikey headed inside, his eyes going wide with wonderment.

"Josie, look! We have a PS5 here!" He screeched, pointing to the control center put under the TV on a rack. "Thus many games!"

I grinned, watching my sibling jump at the CDs stacked at the side and wheeze as he remarked on each title he put his little hands on. It was very... commonplace it was inspiring.

"Seems to be your sibling likes it here," Louis remarked energetically, folding his arms over his chest what's more, resting up against the door jamb.

"Previously... erm, everything... he was somewhat dependent," I shrugged, not certain why I wanted to share. "However, games aside, for what reason did we need to move here? I loved it at Rosalynd's."

"Sure you did," Louis sneered. "Be that as it may, the Inn is utilized to get the untouchables far from the Pack, and both you

furthermore, your sibling are neither outcasts nor is it sound

for you to remain distanced from others. You want to

associate if you have any desire to keep your psychological well-being in

check. Wolves are gregarious creatures all things considered."

"That is simply crazy. I'm not a wolf, nor is Mikey!

Furthermore, you don't have any acquaintance with us. You don't have the foggiest idea what we

could do to you on the off chance that you're not sufficiently cautious."

"Attempt. What you could attempt to do, Josie." Louis remedied,

obviously disregarding the initial segment of my assertion. "However

that is the reason you're here in any case - so I-we can

watch out for you." He added, giving me a wide,

wolfish smile.

I shuddered, however not from dread this time. This time it

was... energy. I felt a surge of adrenaline in my

veins, the thoughtful one would feel while remaining on the

bluff's edge prior to jumping into the tremendous sea. Some part

of me - that new and undesirable part it was challenging to

overlook to an ever increasing extent - was excited. It blossomed with the

quality of risk and certainty that was radiating from

Louis in discernible waves. It pulled me to him...

I unexpectedly licked my lips, and Louis' eyes

obscured as he zeroed in on my mouth. Some way or another, I knew

he needed to kiss me. Furthermore, in the event that I inclined a piece nearer, his lips would just be such a long ways from mine that I could just...

Stand by. What was I in any event, doing?

I made a sound as if to speak, turning away, feeling pink corrupting

my cheeks as I anxiously brushed my hair at the rear of

my head.

"Erm... Do you realize any spot that is searching for an

additional sets of hands?" I asked, attempting to get the picture of

Louis kissing me somewhere far away from me. I expected to zero in on

my daily agenda. I needed to recall that he was awful information.

Louis positioned his head aside, his eyes still dull yet

not really... extraordinary.

"Why? Is it safe to say that you are searching for a seasonal work?"

"Full-time," I rectified, as the intimately acquainted weight

returned on my shoulders. At the rate I was going, I

would transform into a lifter sooner than I would into a

werewolf. Which was very entertaining on the off chance that I truly thought

about it.

"However, you're still in secondary school?" He half-asked, halfstated,
wrinkling his temples in disarray.

"I need to quitter. I really want cash to support both me

what's more, Mikey, don't I?" I chuckled sharply, watching my

sibling fascinated in a game without a consideration in the

world. It was decent that he may as yet keep up with some of

his guiltlessness, notwithstanding everything that had occurred.

"Try not to stress over it. The Pack deals with their own,"

Louis recently shrugged. "Furthermore, I'm certain Da would track down it hostile on the off chance that he heard that you figured he proved unable

accommodate you and Mikey." Seeing my befuddled look,

Louis added. "It's something alpha. Alphas make it a point

of distinction to really focus on their thought process is theirs. Particularly

on the off chance that it concerns children and females. You'll before long get it

what I mean."

"Yet, I'm not your dad's ownership, nor is Mikey. Your

father have zero control over me. No one can. Furthermore, to work

full time and deal with myself and my sibling with

my own two hands, I certain as damnation will. I needn't bother with

anyone's assistance or consent. Certainly not someone's

who played a part in destroying my family," I growled,

exasperated.

"Watch out, Josie," Louis cautioned, his voice abrupt.

"For sure?" I tested seeing his eyes going light

silver.

"Or on the other hand he'll hack my balls off on the preparation later on. What's more,

different folks'." another voice I didn't perceive

unexpectedly hindered us. My head snapped to the side as

my eyes arrived on a more youthful rendition of Louis and Jack.

The kid was around fifteen, on the off chance that I needed to take a harsh

surmise, and had muddled hair that was a tiny bit lighter than

Louis'. He likewise had dim blue eyes encompassed by lashes

each young lady would kill for. "I'm Jonah, coincidentally. This prick's more youthful brother."

"Jonah, habits," Louis mumbled with a moan.

"You know such a word doesn't really exist in my
word reference, right?" The kid, Jonah, bit back as I yelped
out a giggle. "All in all, what's your name, pretty?"

"This is Josie. She'll remain with us for some time, so
act. That implies no going around exposed," Louis
lifted his forehead at his more youthful sibling.

"You're unpleasant, ya dig? In any case, Josie, you don't even
know that I am so glad to at long last have someone with a
vagi... Oof! What was that for?" Jonah shouted,
insulted, grasping the side of his head that Louis
whacked just a second prior.

"Advised you to stay on your best possible behavior. There's a little guy
here,"

The more seasoned of the siblings said as Mikey bashfully
moved toward us, taking cover behind me, his eyes inquisitively
turning the kid upward and down, his noses jerking.

"Huh? Furthermore, who's that little fella?" Jonah mumbled, his
nose imitating Mikey's. It looked strange, to say the
least.

"Mikey, Josie's more youthful sibling."

"Josie has a voice, you know?" I cut in, feigning exacerbation. I
had sufficient of being represented.

"What's more, it's as se..." Jonah's eyes snapped to Louis, previously
zeroing in back on me once more. He hacked. "...I mean as

pretty as your face. Say, do you have a mate yet?"

A low threatening snarl unexpectedly filled the lobby

Chapter 12

Jonah surrendered placatingly and eased off,

zeroing in his sight on the floor while uncovering his exposed

neck to Louis. Mikey began to shudder close to me, and I

consequently side-embraced him, however, honestly, I

didn't give a lot of consideration to the seven-year-old at that

exact second. My emphasis was exclusively on Louis, whose eyes

turned so light dim they nearly appeared to be white.

Eery. Wolf-like. Frightening.

It was whenever I first had seen the person so out of it, and it

creeped me out.

"Apologies, brother, I didn't have any idea. I was just messed around,"

Jonah murmured, gazing hard at the floor, his hands not

indeed, even an inch lower.

Louis shut his eyes, and he grasped the scaffold of his

nose, breathing out delicately.

"Go," Was all he said, his voice an octave lower and

rough.

Frigid.

Jonah shouldn't for a second need to have been told two times. He skedaddled,

practically stumbling over his extremely two feet as they attempted to stay aware of how quick his cerebrum pushed him to get away. It

would have been interesting in the event that the entire circumstance wasn't really

cracking terrifying.

A strained quietness fell upon us, disturbed simply by the

subsiding sound of Jonah's rearranging feet. It went on for a

little while before Louis made a sound as if to speak and

looked at me from the side. His eyes, express gratitude toward God,

gotten back to their ordinary mercury silver.

"Sorry about that," he said timidly, his cheeks colored

with light pink.

"What was in any event, going on with that?" My voice appeared

surprisingly weak. I swallowed, attempting to dispose of the ball that

had stalled out in my throat. I was clearly still a little

stirred up.

"Simply some person's stuff, nothing to stress over," Louis

forgotten about me. It didn't seem don't like anything to stress

going to me, yet I remained quiet about my viewpoints. "At any rate,

I'll pass on you to unload. Supper will be served around

six. Jonah is cooking, so it ought to try and be consumable."

"Right, supper, much appreciated," I said, my temples wrinkling as I

watched Louis, my look still dubious.

"OK, see you around then." He said, stepping back.

"...Yeah, see ya," I mumbled, yet he had previously left.

I shook my head, attempting to disregard the ache that

unexpectedly cut my chest. I ought to likely get utilized

to this strange.

[*]

"Jonah, a word?" Louis thumped softly at the open

entryways prompting his sibling's realm.

To the surprise of no one, the inside of Jonah's room looked like

it was removed directly from Dante's Inferno. Garments,

books, games, and garbage were dissipated in a real sense

all over - mostly, notwithstanding, on the floor. Also, on the off chance that he

looked under the little guy's bed, Louis was certain he would

find jazz mags above numerous different things he liked

not to contemplate comparable to his sibling.

Or on the other hand contact.

Typically, it was his responsibility to rouse the youngster to clean. What's more,

he oversaw fine and dandy without mishandling his

position as the more predominant wolf, more seasoned sibling, or

Master. However, Louis had been so ridiculously occupied recently with

the bodies jumping out like toasts close to their line that

he had no time or heart to pursue the young person. All things considered,

obviously, he expected to.

"No doubt, wazzup?" Jonah asked, hauling Louis out of his

thoughts.

The more youthful kid stopped a game and quickly stood

up from the floor he had been perched on while venting

on the cushion. Clearly, Jonah didn't see the value in his more established sibling approaching above him - his wolf felt helpless in

such a position, particularly while facing a greater

hunter. What's more, typically, Louis' wolf would do everything

to relieve the youngster. The present moment, however, it wasn't precisely

the case. In any case, Louis required his wolf to quit provoking his

brother. He felt regretful enough for treating Jonah so cruelly

just some time prior.

"See, I'm grieved," Louis moaned, resting on the casing. He

was humiliated by his eruption, not that he would

just let it out without holding back. All things considered, he seldom let completely go like

that, and it irritated him.

"See, brother, I'm glad for yourself and all, yet you ought to

have quite recently let me know she's your mate prior to going ballistic

on me. I could never have made a joke like that," Jonah

muttered, pushing his hands in his jean pockets.

Louis felt like he was struck by lightning, his eyes

going wide with shock. He snapped his look to his

sibling, procuring himself a loud chuckle.

"Try not to let me know you didn't understand?" Jonah shook his head,

as yet giggling. "You're truly imbecilic for someone who

lived 50 years, ya know?"

Louis grinned warpedly.

Perhaps he truly was.

[*]

It was Piri chicken for supper - presented with turmeric

flavored broiled rice and salad, and fried fish and French fries for Mikey.

The mind-set was tolerable, basically on the grounds that Jonah was such

a freewheeler remaining nervous with him was hard

around. Thus, after the primary off-kilter ten minutes, I

begun to unwind and, in a matter of seconds, thought of myself as snickering

at the teen's jokes.

However at that point Jack needed to demolish everything.

"In this way, I've heard you're searching for a task, and you need to

go full-time. Shouldn't something be said about school?" He asked, observing

me eagerly from the top of the table.

"Dad..." Louis went against delicately from where he was situated

on the right half of his dad.

At the point when we came for supper, I was some way or another fooled into

sitting close to Louis with Mikey inverse me, and Jonah

pressed between his dad and the seven-year-old. It

appeared Rosalynd was typically around with some

other... individuals. However, today, she had a gathering, and the

rest wasn't welcomed on the grounds that Jack would have rather not made me

or on the other hand Mikey any more awkward than we as of now

were.

However, I certain as damnation felt awkward at this point.

My stomach dropped as I looked at Jack, setting my

fork down on my plate. I had really lost my

hunger.

"All things considered, I somewhat likely exited last week in any case, with our abrupt excursion and so forth. Furthermore, I want to

deal with Mikey now," I made sense of, getting out of the

corner of my eye Louis gesturing marginally at Jonah.

The more youthful kid quickly stood up and waved Mikey to

trail behind him, "Come Munchkin. How about we play

something."

"What? Stand by - " I fought as Mikey excitedly slid

off his seat. Louis' hand arrived on my tight, halting

me in my tracks. My eyes consequently went to his

silver circles, my temple brought up in issue as the glow

spread from his hand up my leg to my, indeed, southern

areas.

I attempted to disregard the inclination, yet I could have recently attempted to

extinguish a woodland fire with a container of water. My mid-region

crushed in delight as my pulse got,

beating 100 miles each hour. I digit within my

cheek, and Louis' eyes obscured with...

Jack made a sound as if to speak, snapping me back to the real world.

Poop. My cheeks became ruby red, conceivably mixing

with every one of the spots littering my face as I hurriedly pushed

Louis' hand off my tight, causing him a deep sense of disappointment and

my alleviation.

Inept chemicals.

"Is this your, what, sophomore year?" Louis' dad

asked without overlooking anything, despite the fact that his eyes were shining with entertainment. It really made him look

the most human I had seen him since our first

experience.

"Senior, really," I revised, and he gestured to himself.

"It's chosen then, at that point. You'll complete school. Furthermore, assuming that you need

to bring in some pocket cash, you can work parttime

either after your classes or on the ends of the week," Jack stood

up, completing the conversation.

Indeed, letting it be known, it was nowhere near finished.

I pushed my seat back, promptly up on my own two

feet, gritting my teeth. "See, I value your anxiety,

yet, Mum has recently unloaded us on you, and I would rather not

inconvenience you for longer than needed."

I really want cash. Me and Mikey need an exit plan. We should

track down individuals with the fix and leave. Perhaps move to

the South Pole in the meantime, as distant from

werewolves and different anomalies as humanly

conceivable. What's more, soon.

Jack grinned, apparently seeing through my ploy. "Don't

stress, Josie. Both of you won't crush our financial plan. We

won't actually feel it."

"B-But-" I attempted again, and by and by, I felt Louis'

hand. This time, in any case, on my fisted hand. He began

to draw little circles inside my wrist with his thumb,

prodding me and diverting me enough that I lost my

energy.

"Whatever else, Josie?" Jack rose his temples at me.

"No, sir," I muttered, breathing out delicately.

"Great. You'll begin coming Monday. Rosalynd has

currently made every one of the important plans, so you

try not to need to stress over anything. What's more, Jonah will help

you track down your strategy for getting around the school. The transport
leaves at

7:45," Louis' dad informed me. "Great night to you

two."

I ground my teeth, making an effort not to detonate with

dissatisfaction. In the future, I would make certain to remain away

from Louis while conversing with his father.

Even better, I would just totally avoid him.

At any rate, it was the ideal opportunity for Plan-B.

Chapter 13

Louis hunkered before the body reviewing the

human's vacant, dead eyes, the declaration of awfulness

always frozen on the defaced face.

"Another?" The Enforcer asked, rage making his

acknowledged and strict passion rise. His wolf needed to

destroy the human, the excess parts at any rate.

Obviously, somebody beat him to the punch. Just the face was left -

for the most part - unblemished. What's more, on the off chance that he needed to make an estimation, it

was just finished so they could recognize the assaulter.

"So it appears. This time, one of them figured out how to make it

past the main line of safeguard, killing Drake before Leigh

heard him and got to him. She's actually squashed about it,"

Raph addressed terribly, his mind-set much more obscure than

normal.

"Fucking trackers," The revile slid through his mouth

before Louis could stop it. His eyes naturally went

to the brunette sitting on the log. She was embracing

herself, her demeanor firm, nails diving in the delicate

tissue of her arms. A curiously large, dark shirt covered

her stripped body - Fallon's, as he absentmindedly took note

- what's more, she was shaking, yet not from cold. Werewolves

were not expose to the impulses of the climate, so it could

just mean a certain something - shock.

Louis let out a low snarl that made Raph snap his eyes

toward him, and Fallon flinch. Leigh gave him a

speedy, anxious look as she licked her lips, her eyes

wild eyed. Louis breathed out, battling to quiet his furious wolf

furthermore, making a respectable attempt not to add to Leigh's tumult.

He abhorred seeing the young lady so defenseless. She barely let

anyone see her powerless side - she was excessively pleased for that.

So the simple idea of Leigh showing any shortcoming

drove his defense into abrogate.

He ran his hand through his hair, wrath bubbling inside

him.

The brunette shouldn't actually be here - she wasn't an

acting fighter. No female was. There were excessively valuable

for that.

"For the wellbeing of God, take the young lady to Rosalynd," Louis woofed

out at Fallon, and the other person quickly followed.

Louis didn't intend to boss him around, however his wolf

was too furious to even consider mindful.

"They certainly find support from some place," Raph

remarked, taking him back to the front and center issue

also, disregarding his little explosion. "Two of them made due

to move away. We lost their tracks close to the stream."

Louis moaned, then, at that point, stood up, feeling the cerebral pain

shaping at his sanctuaries. His dad wouldn't be satisfied.

"Take me there."

[*]

"Get going, Pretty, we're stirring things up around town," Jonah

reported the next morning, busting the entryways

open and pompously giving himself access.

"Definitely, kindly come in. Dislike I'm bare or

anything," I protested, giving the teen an evil stare

while swiftly pulling my shirt down to cover the

remaining pieces of my uncovered stomach.

"Goodness, no doubt, I failed to remember you were a human. Us, werewolves,

couldn't care less about exposure. Everybody has seen

each other in their birthday suit somewhere around once," Jonah

reported unaffected as he strolled in, throwing the vehicle

keys all over for the sake of entertainment. "Hi, Shrimp."

Mikey looked his head out of the restroom and grinned

at Jonah.

"Are you taking Jo some place?" He asked adorably, sitting

on the edge of our twin bed. He began to bob up

also, down on the sleeping pad, the bedsprings squeaking

under him.

"That is no joke," Jonah smiled at my sibling and

unsettled his hair. Mikey smacked at his hand, irritated,

in any case, the teen kid was excessively quick for him, so my sibling

put his tongue out in lieu.

I shook my head, folding my arms over my chest and

scowling at the youngster. "You're accepting I'll consent to
be taken... indeed, any place it is that you need to go."
"The town, I've previously told ya Ms. Irritable. We really want to
purchase garments for you two and whatever
you want for school. The Alpha's requests," Jonah
made sense of quietly, zeroing in back on me and, as a
result, halting exasperating my younger sibling. "Presently
come, we don't have the entire day," He added, getting my
arm. Indeed, he attempted to at any rate. I sneaked past him previously
Jonah could contact me, so rather than my arm, he caught
air. The youngster's eyes extended in shock before his
mouth bended in an evil grin, his irises blazing light
blue.
I could have done without that look.
"Only a bit of tip, Josie," Jonah expressed, crawling toward me
while I stepped back in a state of harmony with his developments.
"Never... run... from... a... wolf..." He began and afterward
out of the blue jumped at me with a cruel speed. I
howled and staggered back, stumbling over my feet as
Mikey snapped to consideration, his look boring openings in
Jonah, who tenderly however solidly folded his hand over
my arm, assisting me with recovering equilibrium before I planted
myself on my butt. "We like the pursuit," Jonah wrapped up,
winking at Mikey, a pompous grin on his high school face.
"Presently, will you happen to your own agreement, or do I want to

drag you out?"

"Goodness, simply push it," I murmured, wriggling myself free
while feigning exacerbation. "I'll come." And put my arrangement into
movement. "Blissful?"
"You have no clue," Jonah answered, previously heading
towards the entryways. "Oy, Shrimp, you comin'?"
Mikey tossed me one final addressing look before he
hurried out after Jonah. I moaned in give up, snatching
my knapsack and tossing it over my arm.
Redforest, here I come.
* * *
"This is cracking mind boggling," I murmured under my
nose, stewing with rage.
It was the third or fourth shop searching for a full-time frame
laborer. However, when I got some information about the real work position,
it worked out that they had an opportunity just for a seasonal worker or no
one by any stretch of the imagination. It was making me loco! I proved
unable
dispose of the inclination that Jack was behind it. He needed to
be. There could have been no alternate way everybody would turn me
down when they saw what my identity was.
I kicked the stone that was lying before me with the
full power of my annoyance and murmured, resting on the hood
of Jonah's dark vehicle. It shocked me that the kid had a
permit by any stretch of the imagination. He didn't look more established
than thirteen, perhaps

fourteen, but then he had really hit his sixteenth

summer two months prior. Perhaps werewolves matured

more slow or something like that. I didn't see numerous older individuals in

In any case, the town.

I crested at the forest in front, folding my arms over

my chest as I trusted that Mikey and Jonah will get back from

the washroom, the vehicle keys hanging in my grasp.

Redforest was about vegetation. Indeed, even the shopping center's little

vehicle leave was encircled by old, emanate trees as of now

washed in all shades of fall. It looked dazzling. Also,

perhaps assuming the conditions were unique, I wouldn't

have disapproved of living here until the end of my life-

"Try not to utter a sound, or I'll shoot."

Or then again perhaps mind-blowingly not.

The gag was diving in the side of my lower back,

my right kidney to be definite. I gradually lifted my hands up,

my heartbeat getting, blood whooshing in my ears as a

little snarl left my mouth.

"Nah-ah. Don't you dare. The weapon's stacked

with silver," a similar rough voice murmured so delicately I

could not have possibly gotten a word he said if not for my

strange hearing.

"Stan, hustle," Another voice participated, more berserk than

the first. "They'll see us any moment now."

Chapter 14

"However, open the ridiculous entryways," Stan requested me, and,
a piece of me was defying the thought, I squeezed the
auto-lock, imploring all divine beings above for somebody to
notice my little risk.

My contemplations floated to Mikey, and I felt better. He, at
least, was protected with Jonah. "Get in, Sweetheart. And negative
tomfoolery. Rich here will pull the trigger previously
you say 'Mummy'."

Goodness, I didn't question that. I took a driver's seat, looking at
expressed Rich in the rearview reflect. He was canvassed in soil
furthermore, grime, and his tangled, earthy colored hair was sticking out
this way and that. I likewise saw his blue eyes appeared
hot and not precisely there. He possessed a scent like blood, and
he was squeezing his passed available to his tight that was
enclosed by the oversoaked wrap. The right one held
a firearm. What's more, it was aimed at my head.

I heard the traveler entryways shutting, and my consideration
moved to the next person, Stan. He confronted me, pointing the
rifle at my liver. He, then again, donned a
broken arm. It stood out at an entertaining point that made my
stomach stir.

I swallowed the bile down.

"Presently leisurely converse and drive us out of the town. On the off chance that I

could do without where you're going, we'll kill you,

comprende?" The man trained, inclining forward so he

wouldn't be noticeable from an external perspective. His unmistakable brown

eyes met mine. "Keep in mind, slow and subtle."

"You realize you have really kidnapped some unacceptable?"

I asked, licking my lips as I gradually put the vehicle in turn around.

The nerves were taking awesome of me, so my leg was

shaking on the grip so damn hard the ride was fairly

uneven. "I'm not the very most unnoticeable individual

at the mo-"

"Quiet down and drive!" Rich burst out, making me flinch in

shock and press the gas pedal with all my psyche. Not

the most brilliant thing to do. The vehicle jumped ahead with a

noisy squeaking clamor. I spun the wheel, attempting my

hardest not to stir things up around town light post. Stan noisily

reviled when he was tossed aside, Rick groaned in

torment while I battled to consistent the vehicle.

"Close your goddamn snare, you cunt! You're focusing on the

young lady out!" Stan yapped at his

companion/partner/buddy. "Also, you, silly, one more

move like that, and the paramedics will be unsticking

your entrails from the entryways, ya hear me?!"

"Distinctly," I swallowed, stressing not to envision my

inner parts on the entryways. I turned right, and we left the vehicle

leave, the truck some way or another all the more consistent under me
now that we hit the principal street.

"Great, drive straight ahead and don't stop except if you're
told to. Nothing troublesome about that, ain't it? We're
leaving this goddamn opening, and assuming you're sufficiently fortunate,
you'll survive it." Stan informed me, actually hunched
down.

Indeed, on the grounds that that was empowering.
I held the wheel more tight, feeling my nails prolonging
furthermore, slicing through the material, my gums oddly
tingling as something in me needed to right away
kill the danger. To divert myself, I looked at Rick.
He was inclining intensely on the rest, his head lolled back,
blood overflowing from his tight down onto the seat.
Jonah wouldn't be satisfied. I glared.

"You sure you would rather not take your companion to the
emergency clinic first? He doesn't look excessively great," I mumbled,
stressed despite everything. I really didn't need
anyone to pass on me, companion or not. I wouldn't stomach
it.

"Close it. He'll be fine," Stan countered, yet that's what he wasn't
persuaded when his eyes immediately dashed to the side to
keep an eye on the person in the secondary lounge. I didn't contend as I
returned my concentration to the street. You for the most part didn't
contend with a person pointing the weapon at your stomach. I digit

within my cheek as my viewpoints got once again to

Mikey. I trusted he would be protected with those bizarre

individuals/werewolves would it be a good idea for anything happen to me. I

trusted he wouldn't miss me that much. I trusted...

An enormous dim dark wolf hopped before the vehicle.

I hit the breaks, quickly spinning the wheel to

stay away from the creature.

We were thrown to the side as I heard the firearm go off and

felt a singing torment in my arm. I shouted out.

Stan hollered something, jumping in the driver's seat.

A tremendous tree arose on my side.

Then, at that point, all I saw was dark.

* * *

There was a murmuring sound coming from the motor. The

driver's entryways were torn on my side, and the cool,

sweet air blended in with the ameliorating smell of woods and

musk drifted to my nose, supplanting the odor of blood

furthermore, exhaust.

"Josie, could you at any point hear me?" A frenzied voice that I dubiously

perceived.

I squinted, attempting to dispose of the fog, my cerebrum all

muddled and soft. I moaned, feeling something wet

streaming down the side of my face. My hand

naturally went to the throbbing spot... furthermore, I cried

out as the burning agony promptly shot through my

right arm. I grasped it, groaning delicately and inclining my

weighty head back on the wheel.

"Shh, it's OK. Try not to move, let me check," The voice

murmured delicately, and solid, delicate hands gradually made a difference

me rest back on the rest. My eyes meandered to the

front seat, a piece bloodied and most certainly empty at this point,

and afterward left, just to meet with mercury spheres.

"Louis?" I flickered, glaring, still somewhat woozy. "What are you doing
here?"

"Gracious, thank fuck," Louis mumbled softly.

"Allow me to get you around here," he said, sliding his arms

under my knees and despite my good faith. He lifted me

up as though I didn't weigh anything, embracing me near his body,

his glow embracing my shuddering structure.

"What occurred?" I asked, attempting to recollect yet

finding it hard to center. "And those two men?"

"Try not to stress over them," Louis snarled horridly, his

eyes eery and light silver. "Allow me to get you home."

I didn't have a home right now, yet I was as well

tired to bring up it. I just rested my head on Louis'

hard chest.

"Master Everton," A profound voice I didn't perceive

hauled me out of Morpheus' grasp.

I lifted my tired eyes and looked at the man in

front. He was tall and wide in a massive manner. He too

oozed power I currently absorbed with Jack and Louis -

dim and hazardous now and again. He had a group cut dull
earthy colored hair, dull earthy colored eyes, and he was exposed as a
day. He was additionally canvassed in blood that was spread
around his mouth. I wouldn't even come close to thinking why.
"Same ones?" Louis asked, his voice without a doubt and
dangerous difficult, his appearance savage. The other person
gestured. "Great, you know what to do."
Yet again the man gestured as he immediately turned
around and jogged towards the forest. I attempted to look
around Louis' shoulders, yet he had no part of that. He
embraced me closer, touching the skin on my arm with
his thumb in a quieting way. After a second, my
oversensitive hearing got the suppressed cries of torment
what's more, asking coming from the forest, be that as it may, I was as well
diverted by Louis to mind as a matter of fact. Whenever he
contacted me, a charming shudder shot through me, and
something in me murmured. I was turning into a pool of mush
furthermore, need. This wasn't like me.
I hacked to cover my shame.
"You can put me down, you know. I'm feeling significantly improved
presently," I said roughly, as Louis continued towards the
vehicle left on the opposite roadside.
Jonah was resting up against the driver's entryways, wearing a
bruised eye that was at that point becoming yellowish-green - all
because of his mending abilities.

"No way," Louis mumbled in my mind, pressing
me delicately, his nose covered in my tangled hair. He was
sniffing me, God even knew why.
"What befell Jonah?" I asked, attempting to change the
subject and occupy myself from Louis' powerful presence.
The young person continued to open the secondary passages.
"Simply siblings' quarrel, nothing to stress over," Louis
gotten over me as he approached the vehicle.
"You gave him a bruised eye?" I asked, confused. He put me
on my own two unstable feet. "Why?"
"Josie, leave it," It was Jonah now. He was strangely serious,
his voice tired. Yet, there was likewise another inclination
looking through. Dissatisfaction.
"Yet, "
"Just... Leave it, please. I deserve it," Was all the
teen said, not even once taking a gander at me, or his
sibling. It concerned me.
"Go," Louis delicately pushed me, finishing my cross examination.
Abruptly, I just felt ridiculously worn out. I murmured, getting
in, my entire body actually shaking. I needed to ball myself
what's more, cry. I presumably ought to.
Louis sat close to me and folded his arm over my
midriff, squeezing me to his warm and ameliorating side. I
sniffed delicately. I was excessively depleted to battle him or feel
humiliated. I just cuddled nearer while Jonah began

the motor.

My eyes felt weighty, so I shut them. Quickly, I floated

off to rest

Chapter 15

"Josie!" Mikey shouted out, running out of the house,

Rosalyn hot behind him.

"Simple, little guy," Louis cautioned, however neither I, nor my sibling

appeared to mind. I hunched and spread my healthy

arm wide separated as the seven-year-old collided with me,

sending me on my base. He pressed my neck so

tight he was removing the air from my lungs, yet I

didn't mind as I cuddled him with my nose, breathing his

soothing adolescent aroma in.

"Alright, Mikey, let your sister go. She really wants to have her

arm checked," Rosalynd said, grinning, despite the fact that I could

see the concern in her golden eyes.

I pated my sibling gently on the back. "You're going to

choke me, Munchkin."

The seven-year-old wasn't irritated. That is until I

begun stifling. He promptly let me go, watching me

eagerly with his green eyes.

"I was frightened," he conceded, and I grinned timidly at

him, unsettling his hair.

"I know. Please accept my apologies, Munchkin."

"Alright, Mikey. Allow me to mind your sister. You can go
with Jonah and have a portion of those hotcakes I've
made," Rosalynd reported, motioning for us to move
into the house. Mikey voiced his endorsement while I gradually
stood up and pursued the lady with Louis just a
breath behind me.
Rosalynd directed me towards my and Mikey's brief
room and afterward to the washroom. The emergency treatment pack was
previously holding up by the sink. She guided me to sit on
the latrine cover as she continued to spread out instruments on the
sink.
Louis rested on the casing, getting his arm over his
chest, for the most part approaching above us.
"What occurred?" Rosalynd began as she took a container
of salicyl liquor and poured it liberally over my
harmed arm. I murmured in torment and snapped my jaw tight.
"It is difficult to make sense of," I snorted once the
burning torment turned into a dull pulse. Louis left his spot
to hunker alongside me. He abruptly took my unharmed
hand, unfisting my fingers and tangling them together
with his. I become flushed, humiliated by his activities, yet I
didn't pull away - his motion really caused me to feel a little
better, intellectually. I trusted Rosalynd had
however, pain relievers some place in her pack. I could
scarcely bear the aggravation as of now, and I realized it was

just the start. "I was sitting tight for Mikey and Jonah

at the point when two people abruptly moved toward me with weapons in

their hands. They were canvassed in mud and were both

harmed. They believed me should drive them out of the town.

One of them was in a real sense draining out on the secondary lounge,"

I reviewed as the bile again rose in my stomach.

Louis crushed my hand - hard. I murmured, snapping my

look to him, and he loosened up his hold a little, however he

would not meet my eyes, his face incomprehensible.

"One of them killed Drake," he remarked gruffly, his

voice absent any trace of any feelings. But then, some way or another, I could

experience his wrath, disappointment, and pity.

"Pause. What?" I shouted once his words enlisted.

"How could they do that?"

Rosalynd tossed Louis a speedy look before she took the

tweezers in her gloved hands. "Since they are

trackers," she mumbled as though it said everything. And afterward, she

just changed the point. "This will hurt. Werewolves are by and large
insusceptible to a wide range of

sedation, so I need to take out the shot without utilizing

any. You can nibble on the material in the event that you need," she
advertised

me a plain, white piece of texture.

That was the point at which I began to overreact.

"Pause. Is it true or not that you will take the projectile at this point? Without
me

taking anything to numb the agony?" I attempted to wriggle
free, having a without a doubt uncomfortable outlook all in all
circumstance.

"I'm apprehensive I have no other decision. I'll attempt to do it as
rapidly and easily as could really be expected, however," Rosalynd
murmured, her demeanor upset however in any case
resolute.

I began to shake my head passionately. "You can't do
that! I disagree. You can't take the shot out without
my assent!"

"There could be no alternate way. Louis, better hold her down," Was all
Rosalynd said as she folded her hand over
my arm.

Louis gave me a conciliatory look before he secured me
his hug. I actually attempted to get free when the first
wave of blinding torment attacked my mind. I proved unable
help the thunder that left my mouth and shook the
washroom's walls. Burning tears began streaming
down my face, filling my mouth with salt. I gritted my
teeth, breathing vigorously through my nose, my nails
prolonging, canines blasting out and busting my lower
lip. And all through that, Louis never delivered his hold,
mumbling romantic things in my hair.

I needed to kill him. I needed to kill those folks who
shot me. I fucking couldn't stand him. I detested them all.

"Nearly there, hun," Rosalynd declared, her voice

stifled by the surge of blood in my ears. I got my

articulation in the mirror - my ordinarily hazel eyes

burning and absolutely golden, face distorted in the

peculiar, brutal way, nostrils erupted. Dabs of sweat

were covering my temple, putting my chestnut hair

to my face and running down my neck. I pressed my

covers tight, petitioning God for all of that to simply fucking wrap up.

However at that point one more shot of agony singed the side of my

arm.

I reestablished my undertakings in breaking myself free as a

wave of adrenaline kicked in, however Rosalynd was as well

solid for me. As was Louis. I began to whine,

asking for them to simply let me go.

"Shh..." Louis mumbled delicately in my mind similarly as

Rosalynd reclined.

"The shot's out, however I need to put on lines. Actually we don't

recuperate too when harmed with silver," She said,

humoring me at the time's rest as she turned

around to set up the fastens. I was gasping vigorously in

my seat by then.

What did I at any point do in my life to acquire this? I never

needed to be a fucking werewolf!

"For this reason your mom needed to leave," Rosalynd

commented startlingly as though guessing what I might be thinking. Then

she confronted me once more, and the virus needle got through

my skin. "She resembled the two people that abducted you.
As was your dad - a tracker. Those fuckers attack
our domains, pursue us with silver slugs and kill us in
the name of their debilitated, antiquated convictions. You recall
this day well the following time you need to call any of us
beasts," The lady completed the bunch and put the
needle away.
"Rosalynd," Louis cautioned, yet she just tossed him a
sharp look.
"Josephine has to know this. She additionally has to be aware
who her folks truly were. This is certainly not a high schooler cleanser
drama. Regardless of whether she prefers it, she needs to begin acting
like one of us to own her relaxing
her most memorable full moon."
I felt debilitated.
"What do you mean?" I asked, feeling the blood channel
from my face.
Louis moaned.
"I think this is a discussion for later," he chose, and
at the point when I opened my mouth to go against, he cut me in.
"Tomorrow, Josie. You had sufficient fervor for
today."
"Anything you wish, Enforcer Everton," Rosalynd gave
Louis a stacked look I was unable to translate and afterward
continued to gather her stuff. "Your arm will be sore at

least for seven days. I'll mind it in four days, however if at

any point you believe you really want me to see, don't

wonder whether or not to come. You know where I reside," Rosalynd

grinned, crushing my knee in consolation. "There's nothing more to it

from my side. I prescribe you to simply rest for now."

With that, the lady stood up and set out toward the

entryways.

"Pause, you can't simply drop a bomb like that and afterward

leave me hanging!" I shouted out as she left. I was

raging. "Furthermore, you," I spun on my heel, confronting Louis

furthermore, sticking his chest with a finger, "Who are you to

let me know the amount I can take?! I'm more than fit

of-"

"Since I can fucking feel them!" Louis half-hollered halfgroaned, cutting me in. "I can feel your ridiculous

feelings, Josie," he added all the more delicately. I ventured away,

totally shocked. I didn't have any idea what to say, so I

essentially watched him run his hand through his hair in

disturbance, feeling my own heart vacillate in my chest. For a

minute there, we both just remained peacefully. However at that point

Louis reviled faintly, convoluted, and

squashed my lips with his.

Louis had never intended to kiss Josie like that.

All things considered, he had really longed for kissing her and doing

other - not precisely respectable - things to her several

times, however he had never expected to kiss her so...

generally. In any case, not the initial time round. Nipping,

sucking, and teeth shouldn't have be involved. He

essentially needed to comfort her. Expected to even. He had

to delete that large number of extraordinary, dim feelings circling around

Josie's heart and mind, driving her to the edge of no

return, where her wolf would most likely yet totally

dominate. He was unable to allow that to occur; not currently, not

during the forthcoming full moon. Not ever.

She was unable to turn wild.

So he just... kissed her. The stars have aligned just right totally

blameless. In any case, his wolf, all things considered, he had his very own
psyche.

Also, desires - destitute minimal jerk.

So when their lips contacted, the fire inside Louis

unexpectedly touched off, or rather, detonated like a furious

firestorm, running hot in his veins, consuming him

from the inside, gobbling up his entire being. His wolf

yelled in delight, needing to guarantee Josie here and

presently. Louis scarcely halted himself then, some way or another

figuring out how to shut down the monster before they did

something inept - like imprint the young lady even before she

had changed.

Chapter 16

In any case, Louis couldn't quit destroying her lips. Nor crushing

her hip so hard he realized he was most likely swelling her -

however honestly, she didn't appear to mind.

He just... couldn't stop it. Not when Josie

answered him so... enthusiastically. Not when she generally

messed his dark shirt in her grasp, pulling him even

closer, disregarding the undermining whimpers of the creases

which were going to break. He could feel Josie's nails

penetrating the material of the attire and his skin. They

drew blood - however he simply didn't a lot of care by then.

Josie bit his lower lip, sucking it hard in her mouth, and

he snarled low in his throat. She then crawled her

tongue inside him, fighting her direction with his. He knew

what her wolf was attempting to do - she needed to state

her predominance, challenge his situation, check assuming that he was

deserving of her time. Of her. Furthermore, he happily answered. He

pulled her hair a piece, calculating her head so he could

extend the kiss, assuming command over it, directing her tongue

where he believed it should be, doing things that evoked

another of those delicate little groans of hers.

The lump in his jeans turned out to be horrendously unmistakable,

awkward. He drove his hips into Josie's tight,

trusting it would fix his beating issue. Actually it didn't. In reality, it turned out to be more terrible. Such a lot of more terrible. Josie answered

promptly to his thurst. The commotion of her pleasure was

again got by his mouth as the fragrance of her excitement

superseded his detects, inebriating him, welcoming him...

He some way or another figured out how to tear his lips away and place his

brow on hers - yet his hand never quit measuring the

back of her head possessively, his other one grasping

her hip while his breath left his mouth in whimsical

shallow jeans.

He woke up, gazing directly into Josie's - splendid

gold, shining, wolf-like... She was winded, just

like him, and the red that flushed her face shaped with

the spots that liberally dabbed her straight nose and

generally pale cheeks.

They weren't pale at this point.

Josie looked exquisite, and her wolf was calling to Louis'

soul. He could feel the mate bond snap around his heart

like a capital punishment. He was ill-fated.

What had he done?

He swallowed, shutting his eyes, attempting to focus himself in

the present.

"W-why?" He got Josie's dry, questionable voice.

"For what reason did you do that?"

Yet again he woke up, meeting hers - hazel

presently. He needed to make sense of, yet he questioned she was prepared for the until the end of time talk, or rather,

indeed, even the demise will not part us. So he went for the presumptuous

rather as he grinned and shrugged his one arm.

"Why not?" Louis made himself step away. One agonizing

step back. Then, at that point, one more as the bond wound more tight

around his spirit. The scourge of God. He pushed his

hands in the pockets of his green freight pants, attempting to

conceal how they shuddered. "You have yourself worked

up. It appeared to be really smart around then."

However, god just knew how inept it was. Josie may

not endure her most memorable shift. There was a 70% opportunity she

wouldn't, which implied he would trail behind

her. He fundamentally shot himself in the foot with

that kiss.

Fuck.

"B-But. You bearly know me!" Josie shouted as she

begun walking forward and backward. "Also, I bearly know you,"

she added as she ran her hand through her somewhat

rumpled, chestnut waves, confounded. Disappointed at

him, presumably at herself that she had completely loved

that kiss.

"So? Why does it make a difference? You've appreciated it, I've delighted in

it. It's a shared benefit," Louis streaked her with another smile

that made her blush become blood red and creep down her

neck. He preferred that variety on her. It did peculiar things to his rooster. "Also, I don't have anything against getting to be aware you better." Louis winked, getting a charge out of how her heart unexpectedly skirted a beat.

"You know what, Louis? I believe you're correct. I've had enough energy for one day," Josie chose suddenly, spinning on her heel. "Gratitude for saving my life what not in any case, just... leave."

She was obviously excusing him. It didn't stage him one bit since he could detect she needed to invest some energy into it. He chose, nonetheless, he would allow Josie to have her way - until further notice. Thus, he just grinned the grin he knew was savage and promising. It drew her wolf out once more - her eyes streaked golden.

"Of course, Josie," Louis expressed unbothered as he headed for the entryways. "I'll let myself out."

The game was on.

* * *

I breathed out a breath I didn't realize I was holding and amassed vigorously on the latrine cover.

Poo, poo, shit~!

I kissed Louis. All things considered, essentially, he kissed me, yet I answered back and enthusiastically, and I even groaned, and, gracious God, for what reason did I need to effing groan?!

I shut my eyes, feeling humiliation slithering down my skin like liquid magma. I was so confounded I didn't

understand what to do any longer. First my folks, then, at that point, the
grabbing, then this happens...

I let out a boisterous breath that made a portion of my hair fly up
furthermore, away from my temple. Perhaps I wanted a therapist.
Or on the other hand a jug of vodka. Make it two.
I scoured my face with my healthy hand. Essentially the
kiss filled in as an interruption. Essentially I figured out that
Louis was intrigued, perhaps felt a similar unusual
pull, the very fire that was consuming inside me when our
lips contacted...
I expected to quit mulling over everything. We were unable to occur. I
didn't maintain that we should occur. I needed to get Mikey and run
for slopes, where no one could track down us, particularly those
trackers.
Jesus.
I stood up and sprinkled my face with cold water. I had
to converse with Rosalynd. She was by all accounts the one to focus on
ready to let me know anything. What's more, I expected to comprehend
what on earth was happening with me, with those trackers,
my folks, and Louis. I detested being in the blue.
I held the sink and checked out at myself in the mirror,
not entirely settled.

    Thank you for reading

THE END